HONOR VALLEY HOLIDAYS

VOLUME ONE

SHANAE JOHNSON

THOSE JOHNSON GIRLS

SHANAE JOHNSON

Love on a Reindeer Run

HONOR VALLEY HOLIDAYS

CHAPTER ONE

*T*he smell of baking gingerbread filled the community center. It was a tantalizing holiday scent that normally would have made Joy Evergreen's heart swell with, well, joy. Today, those familiar smells only tightened the knot in her stomach as she studied the ledger before her. Numbers didn't lie, and the figures were dire.

"Budget cuts again?" Holly, Joy's cousin and very first friend, which made her the very best friend, sighed as she eyed the worry creasing Joy's forehead.

The military base in Honor Valley had been hit with significant budget cuts during the last couple of months. The reductions were affecting various aspects of daily operations, from training to maintenance, and unfortunately, it was now also impacting the support services the base provided to the families living there.

The base's commander was working to find solutions, to reallocate resources where he could. But some services were being limited for the time being. It looked like the annual toy drive was one that was going to take a hit.

Joy looked up to her cousin, whose hands were splattered in sweet-smelling flour, and forced a smile. "It's going to be a challenge, but I'm going to make it work. I have to, especially for the kids on the base. They deserve a magical Christmas."

This wasn't the first time Joy would have to make do with less. Back in high school, Joy, along with Holly and their other cousin and first friend Felice, had learned that the kids on the military base didn't do Christmas quite like the Evergreens. Joy's family owned the town Christmas tree farm as well as a year-round holiday store that sold Christmas items even on Halloween and Easter. Having anything less than the Evergreen holiday experience was unimaginable to the Evergreen girls, and so they decided to do something about Christmas on the base.

Felice, who had the voice of an angel, organized a caroling event every year for the base families. Holly, who could bake like no one's business, organized the food drive as well as a holiday dinner for the families. And Joy took charge of the toy drive.

Inside the base's recreation center, the room was adorned with garlands and sparkling fairy lights that were now turned off. Only thirty minutes ago, the children had been sitting at the tables, eating gingerbread and penning letters to Santa. Their happy faces had lit up, asking for gifts Joy wasn't sure she could provide.

"Those families are already under enough stress with the deployments," Joy said, her voice thick with emotion. "The children shouldn't have to feel the pinch of budget cuts. Christmas is about hope, joy, and love. I can't let them down."

"You won't. You never do." Holly's assurance was sincere, but Joy couldn't shake the worry.

Outside the window, snowflakes danced on their trip from the clouds, adding to the festive atmosphere. Joy's heart felt as cold as the snow. How could she tell those children that Santa might not come? Their families were sacrificing so much for the country, and the least she could do was give them a joyful holiday.

She had a budget. She'd just make it stretch.

With the rec room cleared of pens, paper, and gingerbread crumbs, Joy and Holly parted ways.

Back in her apartment, Joy settled into the cozy armchair by the twinkling lights of her Christmas tree. She held a steaming cup of hot cocoa in one hand and a stack of children's letters to Santa in the other.

The children's wishes were simple. Most of the letters were filled with dreams of toys and pets. But there were also poignant reminders of the reality they faced, wishes for deployed parents to remain safe while they were away.

Then she came across a letter that stopped her in her tracks. It was written in a careful, mature hand that belied the age of most of the elementary-aged children that had been present today.

"Dear Santa," the letter began, "I'm writing this for my little brother, Jamie. He's too young to write, but he told me what he wants. He wants the Star Voyager action figure. I know it's hard to get, but he really wants it."

The sister was right. The Star Voyager action figure was the season's hottest item. Surprisingly, none of the other children had asked for it. This letter was the first to request the toy.

"But I know you're not the real Santa. I know this is just an adult reading this. If you were real, all I would ask for is my mom to come home for Christmas. She's a soldier who's fighting for our country. Me and Jamie miss her so much. So on the chance that you're real, can you please grant my wish and bring my mom home for Christmas?"

The letter was signed by Amber and Jamie.

Joy's hand trembled as she put the letter down, her heart aching for the children and their longing for their mother. She couldn't bring their mother home, but she would find that toy. She would bring a little magic into their lives. If she could grant just one wish, make one child's dream come true, then she'd have captured the spirit of Christmas.

Her mind raced, thinking of ways to find the elusive Star Voyager action figure. She knew it wouldn't be easy, but she was resolved to do whatever it took. She also knew exactly whose help to seek to find a lead on the toy.

Joy sent out a text and then headed to Sandy Perk, the coffee shop near the beach. The aroma of freshly ground coffee beans filled the air, blending with the chatter of patrons and the soft hum of steaming milk. Her cousins Felice and Holly had already arrived and had her hot cocoa in hand.

"What's going on?" asked Felice.

Joy took a deep breath, her fingers tracing the rim of her mug. "I read this letter from a little girl today. She wrote to Santa for her brother but ended it saying that all she wanted was for her mom to come home from overseas."

"That's heartbreaking," said Holly.

"It is," Joy agreed. "But it's also inspiring. I've decided to find that toy for her brother. I want to make their Christmas special."

"That's so like you, Joy," Felice said, her voice filled with pride. "Always thinking of others."

"What can we do?" asked Holly.

"Help me figure out where to find a Star Voyager action figure."

Both her cousins' smiles fell. Joy held on to hers. She knew it would be hard, but these were two of the most positive and tenacious women she knew. If they couldn't help her, no one could.

Joy's smile did falter when she caught sight of her boyfriend, Mark, standing outside the coffee shop window.

Holly smirked when she caught sight of him. "You sure he doesn't have one of those toys stashed under his bed in his mom's basement?"

Both Holly and Felice thought Mark was an overgrown kid. Joy didn't disagree. She wasn't looking for anything serious. With his job at the movie theater, the same popcorn-slinging job he'd had since middle school, Mark was as unserious as they came.

Mark waved at her through the window. Joy waved back. Holly and Felice both showed him their teeth. Mark recoiled.

"Think about where I could get that toy while I talk to him," Joy said before heading out.

"Hey, babe."

Joy gritted her teeth. She hated being called babe. She'd told this to Mark more than once. He only seemed able to retain information for a few hours before it went out the other ear.

"I've got great news," he went on.

It was likely that the theater had gotten an early copy of the latest blockbuster. Or perhaps a new video game had just dropped. It didn't take a lot to get Mark excited.

"I got a promotion."

Joy's smile wavered. "You got a what?"

"I'm going to be the assistant manager at the movie theater. Isn't that great?"

"Wow. Yeah. I never knew you had any ambition for... that."

"Now I'll be in charge of making schedules. If a piece of equipment breaks, I have to call the technician. Oh, and I'll have to do inventory every Friday night, so that might cut into our Netflix and chill time."

"That's great, Mark," she said, her voice steady but distant. Her heart thumped loudly, echoing the same rhythm it had years ago when another guy had said similar words—right before leaving her for new opportunities. Joy felt like she was on the precipice of a cliff, staring down into an abyss of repeating history.

"I've been thinking. We're on different paths. I need to focus on what's important to me, on the people and causes I care about."

Mark's face fell, his eyes widening with disbelief. "Are you breaking up with me?"

"I think it's for the best. Now you can focus on your promotion and your new responsibilities."

Mark looked at her in disbelief. But she knew she was making the right decision. Joy turned away from him, away from the coffee shop, and headed home. Her footsteps were light, but her heart heavy as she faced the chilly evening air.

A pang of regret twisted in her gut. She steeled herself against it, guided by a painful lesson from her past. Once, when ambition had beckoned, her heart had paid the cost. It was a price she was no longer willing to pay.

CHAPTER TWO

*L*ucas Jackson stood outside the weathered gates of the elementary school. It looked smaller than when he had been enrolled in Honor Elementary. The familiar sight of the playground tugged at memories buried deep within him.

The metal swing set creaked gently in the wind. The worn wooden benches told stories of laughter, games, and innocence. He could almost hear the sound of young children's voices mingling with the distant rustle of leaves. Louder than those sounds were the echoes of a time when he and Joy had claimed this playground as their own world.

Joy.

Just her name brought a rush of emotions, a flood of memories. She had been bossy, always telling him what games to play, which trees to climb. Lucas had loved every minute of it. He had loved being bossed around by her, loved the sparkle in her eyes when she was in command.

He wandered closer to the swing set. His hand reached out to touch the cold metal chain. The sensation stirred a vivid memory of Joy's hand in his, her laughter filling the air.

They had dated through middle and high school, two young hearts intertwined, promising each other forever. He had thought he would spend the rest of his life with her. The future had seemed so certain, so full of promise. Then the military had come calling.

His career had pulled him away. The military had offered opportunities, responsibilities, and a path that he felt he needed to follow. In doing so, he had left Joy behind, breaking both their hearts.

Five years later, he could still see the tears in her eyes, the confusion and betrayal. He could still hear her voice, trembling with emotion, asking him why. Why was he choosing his career over their love? Why was he walking away?

Lucas's chest tightened, a lump forming in his throat as he wrestled with the old guilt, the lingering questions. Had he made the right choice? Had he traded true love for ambition?

He shook his head, forcing himself back to the present. The playground was empty now, the laughter and voices long gone. But the memories remained, etched into every corner, every piece of equipment.

With a sigh, he turned and walked away, the past receding behind him. But he knew those times would never leave him. The love he had shared with Joy, the dreams they had built together, would always be a part of him, a bittersweet reminder of what might have been.

Lucas was lost in thought, the ghosts of the past still lingering in his mind, when a sudden shout broke through his reverie. "Uncle Lucas!" a young voice called, filled with surprise and excitement.

A little boy ran toward him, his face lit up with excitement. Behind him, a slightly older girl followed, her eyes pinched at the edges in tolerance.

"Jamie? Amber?" he stammered, his mind struggling to reconcile the small, familiar faces with the years that had passed.

"Uncle Lucas!" Jamie threw himself into Lucas's arms with complete abandon.

Lucas caught up his small body and hugged him

tightly. He felt the warmth and energy of the young boy, the innocence and trust that still shone in his eyes.

"Hi, Uncle Lucas," Amber said, more reserved. A small smile touched the edges of her eyes, releasing the pinched look for a fraction of a second. "We missed you."

"I missed you too, kiddos. I missed you both so much."

Lucas knelt down to look at them more closely, taking in the changes, the ways they had grown and matured. Jamie's hair was a bit darker, and his face had lost its baby roundness. Amber's eyes held a wisdom beyond her years, a reflection of the challenges they had faced.

"You look just like your dad," Lucas told Jamie, his heart aching at the memory of his brother, gone too soon.

Jamie's face fell for a moment, a shadow passing over his eyes, but then he looked up, hopeful. "Is Mommy here too?"

Lucas felt a pang of sadness, knowing the disappointment that awaited. "No, Jamie, not yet. But she'll be home soon."

"When?" Amber asked, her voice tinged with longing.

"Soon," Lucas repeated, wishing he could give them a more definite answer. "She's still deployed, but she'll be back as soon as she can."

The children's faces fell, their excitement dimming, but Lucas was determined to lift their spirits. "Guess what? I've been permanently assigned to the base here in Honor Valley."

"Really?" Jamie's eyes sparkled again. "You're staying?"

"Yes," Lucas confirmed. "I'm staying. I'll be here to take care of you and to be with you."

The promise was more than just words; it was a commitment, a pledge to be there for them, to fill the void left by their father's passing and their mother's absence.

"See, Amber? I told you Santa was real. But he's old. So that's why he sent us Uncle Lucas instead of Mom. But I'm happy Uncle Lucas is here. I'm going to write another letter. Will you help me this time, Uncle Lucas?"

Those were a lot of words to digest. Lucas was used to the baby Jamie babbling incoherently. It took him some time to unravel the meaning.

"Amber doesn't believe in Santa anymore." Jamie regarded Lucas with wide, serious eyes.

"She doesn't?" Lucas asked, trying to keep his voice light. "Why not?"

"Because I asked Santa to bring Mom home last year, but he didn't," Amber said.

"Well, maybe Santa knew that I could help take care of you and your brother while Mom's away."

Amber met her uncle's eyes. Her eyes were so like her father's. Lucas was used to looking into those sure eyes while getting advice. Now he was the one who had to give it.

"No, Uncle Lucas," Amber said quietly. "There's no Santa. If there was, Mom would be home, and Jamie would get the Star Voyager toy he wants. But none of that's going to happen."

Lucas felt a pang of helplessness, knowing that there was nothing he could do to bring their mother home. But the mention of the toy, the Star Voyager, sparked an idea.

"Well, Santa is a toy maker, so I'm sure he'll get your toy, Jamie."

Lucas knew that he had made a promise, one that he was determined to keep. Not just for Jamie's sake, but for Amber's as well, to show her that there was still magic in the world, that miracles were possible.

The Star Voyager toy was more than just a play-thing; it was a symbol, a way to restore faith and joy, to bring a touch of magic back into their lives. And Lucas was ready to do whatever it took to make that happen, to give them a Christmas filled with love and hope, and to prove that Santa was real, in one way or another.

CHAPTER THREE

*J*oy pulled into the crowded parking lot of the bustling shopping center in the nearby town. The tip she'd received was a golden opportunity, but it seemed that she wasn't the only one in pursuit of the elusive Star Voyager toy. A long line of determined adults, eyes gleaming with a blend of anticipation and desperation, snaked around the building, leading to the entrance of the toy store.

The sharp chill of the morning air nipped at her cheeks as she joined the line, the smell of fresh snow mixing with the aroma of coffee from a nearby café. She could hear the murmur of tense conversations, the shuffle of feet, the restless energy of the crowd.

"I heard there's only a dozen left," someone said, panic edging their voice.

"We've been here since dawn," another grumbled, wrapping their arms around themselves for warmth.

Joy's stomach twisted with anxiety, the weight of the promise she'd made to the little boy pressing down on her. Yes, it had been a silent promise, but she knew that Santa had heard her.

To her and every Evergreen, Santa was more than a jolly old man. He was an idea, one that had to be reinforced. And to do that, the idea needed to be fed by the belief of little children. That Star Voyager toy would reignite the belief of not just one but two children. It was a symbol of hope, a way to keep the magic of Christmas alive.

The bottom line: Joy had to get her hands on one of those toys.

The moment the doors to the toy store creaked open, all semblance of order and decorum vanished. What was once a line of patiently waiting parents and guardians transformed into a frenzied stampede, a riotous surge of limbs, shopping carts, and frantic voices. The race for the Star Voyager toy was on, and it was a sight to behold.

In the midst of the chaos, an elderly grandma, her body bent and her legs creaky, suddenly dropped her cane, her eyes fixed on the prize. With a surprising burst of speed, she shot forward, her floral dress flapping behind her like a superhero's cape. Grandma darted past a muscular father, his face red with effort as he stumbled over his own feet.

A woman with frazzled hair and her glasses askew tripped over a wayward shopping cart, only to be hoisted up by a kind-hearted young man. The two of them locked eyes for a brief, romantic moment before resuming their mad dash.

A man in a business suit, his tie flapping wildly, tried to maintain his dignity as he stepped on some-one's handbag, only to slip and land in a heap of garish holiday sweaters.

"Excuse me, pardon me!" a woman squealed, hopping over the fallen businessman, her arms flailing like windmills as she fought to keep her balance.

The whole scene was pure chaos of colliding bodies, clashing carts, and wild determination, all set to the cheerful jingles of holiday tunes playing over the store's speakers. There was something almost magical about it, a comical dance of desire and desperation, a shared mission that united them all in a frenzied rivalry.

At the heart of it all was the Star Voyager toy, a

symbol of dreams and wishes, a beacon of joy, a status symbol of how much a child's adult loved them that brought out the competitive spirit in everyone assembled.

"Hey, watch it," Joy cried out as an elbow jabbed into her side. The warmth of bodies pressed against her. The noise rose to a fever pitch.

"I'm sorry," her would-be assailant gasped, their face flushed with urgency. "I just need to get one for my son."

"I understand," Joy panted, fighting to keep her balance, her emotions a whirlwind of frustration, determination, and sympathy.

As she stumbled into the store, the bright lights and colorful displays momentarily disoriented her. She heard the fevered shouts, the clatter of shopping carts, the desperate pleas of parents on a mission.

Joy's eyes darted around, scanning the shelves. Her breath caught in her throat as she spotted it. It glinted like a beacon of hope: one Star Voyager toy left, tucked away in a corner.

Her heart soared, a rush of triumph sweeping through her. She pushed through the chaos. Her mind was focused on her goal. The world narrowed down to that one precious object.

The Star Voyager toy seemed to call to her, a

promise of happiness, a chance to make a child's dream come true. As she reached out to grab it, her fingers trembling with excitement and relief, she knew that she had succeeded.

Time seemed to slow as her hand neared the box. Her fingers stretched, aching to grasp the precious toy. Every sense was heightened—the distant chatter of shoppers, the musky scent of cologne from a nearby clerk, the cool feel of the store's tile beneath her feet dimming as she focused on her singular goal.

As her hand closed around the box, another hand met hers. Joy looked up, her gaze locking on to a familiar pair of deep blue eyes. Eyes she had lost herself in a thousand times before. Eyes that still haunted her dreams.

"Lucas?" she whispered, her voice trembling with surprise and something more fragile, something like longing.

"Joy," he said, his voice warm, his eyes crinkling at the corners as he smiled.

The world around them fell away as memories washed over her. Memories of laughter and love. Memories of promises made and promises broken.

Her hand slipped from the box. Her fingers lost their grip. Her heart lost its footing.

Lucas's hand fell away, too. His fingers tightened around hers instead of the box. His heart was in his eyes as he smiled brightly at her.

He smiled at her like he had when he'd pushed her on the swing, high enough that she'd thought she was flying. He smiled at her like he had after they'd shared their first kiss after the middle school Sadie Hawkins dance when she'd demanded he take her. He smiled at her like he did the first time he told her he loved her after dropping her home just one minute before curfew when they were in the tenth grade.

And then his smile began to fade. His gaze fell away from hers. She yanked her hand away from his, but it was already too late.

With a triumphant laugh, a stranger dashed between them, snatching the last Star Voyager toy from the shelf and disappearing into the crowd.

CHAPTER FOUR

*T*he loss of the Star Voyager toy was inconsequential. The presence of Joy, the way her eyes widened and softened as they met his, filled Lucas with a sense of longing and, well, joy. When she snatched her hand from his, he let her go because he was so focused on not grabbing her to him bodily and pressing her curves into the empty shelves and kissing her senseless like he'd dreamed of doing every single day since the last time he'd seen her.

The noisy clamor of holiday shoppers and the bright and festive decorations of the toy store faded. The surprise in her eyes, the subtle parting of her lips was all too familiar. A wave of emotion washed over him, the memories of their past flooding back with an intensity that left him breathless.

She was just as beautiful as he remembered. Her eyes were still filled with that fire. Her voice still carried that bossy tone that he had always found so endearing.

"What are you doing here?" she demanded.

That was fascinating. Lucas hadn't forgotten the sound of her voice. It rang just as smoky and deep. There was the bite of command to it that he craved from only her. Oh, how he missed having her boss him around.

He wanted her to tell him to hold her, to kiss her, to never let her go. It was an order he'd happily obey. He would stand in the line of fire for this woman. Unfortunately, he might have to duck soon because her eyes were shooting daggers at him.

"I could ask you the same," Lucas found himself saying, his eyes searching hers, a smile playing at his lips. "It's been a long time, Joy."

"A very long time."

The world fell away. The chaos of the store, the cacophony of holiday shoppers, all faded into nothingness. It was just them, two souls reconnecting, reliving the heat of a love that had never quite died.

So why was she turning her back on him and marching away?

"I can't believe you," she hurled over her shoulder. "You made me lose it."

"Lose it?" Lucas asked, easily falling into step beside her.

"I lost the last Star Voyager toy. I needed that for the toy drive," she scolded, her irritation clear.

A chuckle escaped his lips. The sound of her voice, the way she held her head high, like an indignant princess—no, not a princess. Joy was destined to be a queen. How had he let her slip away? How had he allowed the distance, the time, the circumstances to come between them?

"Don't laugh," she snapped. "This is serious. Those kids at the base are depending on me."

The playfulness in his eyes gave way to understanding, a softness that he hoped would convey how much he cared. "You're still doing the toy drive?" he said, reaching out, wanting to bridge the gap between them. "I know how much this means to you."

Her reaction, the way she pulled back, the way she seemed to be fighting against her own emotions, it all struck a chord within him. The tension between them was palpable, the unspoken words, the lingering desire. It all hung in the air, a testament to what they'd once been.

"Can we get a coffee and talk?" There was so much he wanted to say, so much he needed to know about the last five years that had passed between them.

"Coffee?" Her reaction was a jolt, a sudden storm clouding her beautiful eyes. "Coffee, Lucas? After everything?"

The chill in her tone was a splash of icy water. Lucas struggled to comprehend what he was hearing. "Joy, I—" he began, but she cut him off.

"You left me. You dumped me for a job promotion."

The memories from that flooded back. He'd made it a point not to dwell on the last time they'd been together. But the bitterness of that day, the weight of what he'd done, settled heavily on his shoulders. He couldn't blink away the pain in her eyes, the betrayal he'd seen reflected back at him, the hurt and anguish he knew he'd put there.

"Joy, I never meant to hurt you," he said, his voice raw with regret. "I thought it was the best thing for both of us at the time. I thought—"

"You thought wrong," she snapped, her anger a palpable force that pushed him to take a step back.

"You made a choice, Lucas. You chose your career over me, over us."

The words were a blow, a sharp reminder of the decision that had cost him everything. The mall noise receded, leaving only the two of them and the painful silence that stretched between them.

Lucas reached out to her, desperate to connect, to make her understand. Joy jerked away, her body language a clear rejection.

"I can't do this, Lucas."

That was curious. There had been a time where even air struggled to get between the two of them. Now there was a wall between them, palpable and thick. It stretched higher and higher with each passing second. He had to find a way to tear it down. But just as he was about to reach out to her, to try to bridge the gap between them, the sharp chime of an alert on their cell phones cut through the silence.

Joy looked down first. The lift of her brow and tug at the corner of her mouth raised his hackles. Lucas looked down, and a jolt of excitement shot through him.

Last night, he'd signed up on a website for seekers of the Star Voyager toy. A notification about a new delivery flashed across his phone. The wide-eyed look on Joy's face told him she'd seen it too.

"We could work together, you know," he found himself saying, a desperate need to connect with her driving the words from his mouth. "Team up, make sure we both get what we need."

Joy's face iced over in real time as she regarded him. The lack of warmth was like a physical blow. "I don't need your help."

Lucas watched her go, his soul crying out to her, begging her to turn back, to give them a chance. But she didn't look back. She didn't pause. She didn't falter.

The chase for the toy was on. But Lucas knew that it was so much more than just a game. It was a battle for her heart, a battle he was determined to win. No matter the cost.

CHAPTER FIVE

*J*oy slammed the car door, frustration and confusion roiling inside her. Seeing Lucas had shaken her to her very core. Being that close to him had reignited feelings she thought she'd buried deep. Her hands trembled as she fumbled with the keys, desperately trying to fit them into the ignition.

The car refused to start and aid her in a swift getaway. The engine sputtered and died, again and again. The noise of failure, like the taunting laughter of fate, only added to her growing desperation.

Joy hit the steering wheel with the palms of both hands. Tears of frustration threatened to spill over. Her emotions were a mess. She felt trapped, overwhelmed, unable to escape the maelstrom of longing and regret that had been awakened by Lucas's presence.

She could still feel the heat of his gaze, the gentle touch of his hand, the sound of his laughter. It was all too much, too soon, too real. She needed to escape, to get away, to find some space to breathe and think and feel. But the car refused to cooperate, trapping her in a prison of metal and glass, a cage that closed around her with each failed attempt to start the engine.

The scent of burning oil filled the air, a bitter reminder of her failure, both mechanical and emotional. The sound of holiday music drifted from a nearby store, a cruel juxtaposition to her turmoil. Joy's chest ached with the effort to hold back the tears, her throat tight with unspoken words, her heart heavy with the weight of the past.

A knock on the window jolted her from her misery. She looked up to find Lucas peering in the driver's side window. There was concern etched on his handsome face.

She had seen every emotion possible on this man's face. Surprise, delight, anger, frustration, devastation, sorrow, and love. She'd been there for all of them. Caused many. Soothed others.

As he gazed down at her now, a fresh wave of emotion crashed over Joy. She knew that look. That look was the last thing she'd seen when she went into his open arms to seek comfort. All she had to do was reach out.

Joy turned away. She had to. She couldn't face him with tears pricking her eyes and a lump in her throat.

"Need a ride?" he asked, his voice gentle.

She hesitated, torn between the need to escape and the desire to stay. She didn't have the luxury of selfishness. There were too many kids counting on her.

She collected herself and her purse and opened the door. "Just remember, we're on different sides when we get to the store."

Lucas smiled, a warm, genuine smile that reached his eyes and tugged at her heart. "Deal," he said, offering her his hand.

It was a force of habit. That's the only reason she took it. Once upon a time, it had been the most natural thing in the world. Lucas appeared, and Joy took his hand.

It was a mistake. The moment her flesh met his, she felt a spark. That fire had never died. It had always been there beneath the surface, just waiting for a reason to reignite.

One thing was clear: She wasn't over him. Not by a long shot. The past was still alive, still calling to her, still pulling her toward a future that she hadn't dared to imagine.

But that would have to wait. Right now, the toy was the goal. As they drove away, Joy felt a thrill of anticipation, a sense of excitement and hope that she hadn't felt in a long time. Lucas was back in her life, and everything had changed.

Joy sat rigidly in the passenger seat, her guard firmly in place. Lucas's presence was an electric current in the air, charging the confined space of the car. She felt his gaze on her, but she was determined not to let him in.

She pulled out her phone, desperate for a distraction. She thought of texting Felice or Holly but in the end, decided against it. This would have to be a face-to-face conversation over a large mug of hot chocolate with extra marshmallows. She might even have to go into her peppermint stash.

Joy pulled up the website she'd signed up on for notifications about the Star Voyager toy. It was a good ploy that had paid off. A new alert was posted about an online auction for the elusive toy. She'd still go in and try and claim a toy at the new location, but this auction would be backup.

"What's that?" Lucas asked, his voice casual but his eyes sharp, watching her.

"Nothing," Joy replied, her voice tight, her fingers flying over the screen as she placed a bid.

"Come on, Joy, talk to me."

"I'm busy," she snapped, her eyes glued to the screen as the bids climbed higher and higher.

"You can't hide behind that screen forever. We need to talk about what happened, about us."

"There is no us. There's only the toy, the goal, the end."

"You don't believe that."

She didn't. For more than half her life, she had been an *us*. Her name was rarely spoken without Lucas's. *Joy and Lucas are on the playground. Joy and Lucas are out at the movies. Joy and Lucas are the cutest couple.*

"I had a boyfriend."

"Had?" Lucas pounced on the word, his voice triumphant, his eyes gleaming. "Not have?"

She hadn't meant to use the past verb, but there had never been any secrets between her and Lucas. She looked up then. Her eyes met Lucas's. She knew she was caught, trapped, exposed. "I've had many."

Lucas didn't like that answer any more than the flubbed one.

Joy didn't want to get into the reason why she'd had a revolving door of boyfriends who'd barely lasted longer than a loaf of bread. Her heart was a jumbled mess as she sat beside him in the too-small Ford truck.

His proximity was maddening. The scent of his cologne filled her senses. Memories of their past tugged at her heartstrings. She tried to focus on her mission, the reason behind her desperate need for the toy. Which led her to try another ploy.

"I'm getting that Star Voyager toy for a toy drive. I promised I would. You should help me get it instead of competing against me."

"I wish I could, Joy. But I have responsibilities of my own now."

Responsibilities? Was there someone else in his life now? A child, perhaps? The thought sent a pang shooting through her that would have had her doubling over if not for the seatbelt.

They pulled up to the store. Joy saw the chaos inside through the windows. The desperate shoppers were already fighting over the remaining toys.

"I have to go," she said. "I have to get that toy."

"Joy, wait," Lucas called out, reaching for her arm.

She was already out of the car, the door slamming shut behind her. She raced into the fray, her mind focused on her goal. But her heart was still aching, still yearning for that *us* that had always been there for more than half her life. She left the other half of herself behind and went into battle alone.

CHAPTER SIX

*L*ucas watched Joy spring out of the car. He sat there for a moment and admired her lithe form moving with purpose and grace as she headed into the fray. He could have chased after her, matched her stride for stride, but something held him back. He knew in his gut that she needed this head start, this moment of independence, but he had no intention of letting her slip through his fingers again.

As she disappeared into the crowd, her long hair flowing behind her like a battle flag, Lucas's hand found his phone. He glanced at the online auction he had found for the Star Voyager toy. The last bidder had bid high, too high. They must really want this toy. But so did he, and not just the toy. He increased his bid, his fingers steady and certain as he tapped the screen.

The truck's leather seat creaked as he shifted to get out and join the melee. Outside, the sounds of laughter, chatter, and the distant cry of a street vendor created a cacophony that seemed both distant and immediate. The world was moving around him, but Lucas felt strangely still.

Joy had or had had a boyfriend. The way she'd said it, the slight catch in her voice, the flicker of emotion in her eyes had told him everything he needed to know. It told him that that boy didn't matter. Not to him. What mattered was the here and now, the connection they still had, the fire that still burned between them.

As he watched the numbers on the auction rise and fall, the tension in his body grew. He kept one eye on the auction and the other on the frenzy at the storefront. The seconds ticked down, and the bids climbed higher and higher. Lucas was in it to win it. Not just the toy, not just the auction, but Joy herself. Her heart, her trust, her love.

He upped his bid again. It was just in time. The auction ended, and Lucas grinned down at the screen.

He had won. The Star Voyager toy was his. But the real prize, the real victory, was still out there, still waiting, still... Was Joy climbing over another person to get farther up in the line?

With a smile, he pocketed his phone and stepped onto the battlefield.

He lost sight of her for a second. But then he spotted her. Joy's face was set in determination, her body poised for action. Without a second thought, he dashed into the fray, his body moving with a grace and power that was as natural as breathing.

The air in the toy store was electric with the frenetic energy of last-minute holiday shopping. The fluorescent lights overhead cast a stark glow on the sea of frenzied parents and guardians. Their faces were all twisted in a mix of hope and desperation. Christmas carols played over the store's sound system, but the songs were almost entirely drowned out by the cacophony of shouted conversations, squealing children, and the thundering of footsteps.

In the midst of the swirling chaos, Lucas stood, his eyes locked on to the last Star Voyager toy set perched precariously on the top shelf. It was as if he had blinders on. The world around him dissolved into an indistinct blur, and all that remained was the prize.

He saw the obstacles in Joy's path—the people, the displays, the chaos. One by one, he moved them aside, making the way easier for her, guiding her without her even knowing it.

Lucas saw a dad taking a step toward the shelves. It looked as though the dad was about to shove Joy out of his way. Lucas's protective instincts flared.

With an agility that belied his size, Lucas wove through the crowd. He passed in front of the dad and spun the man in the other direction, which allowed Joy to move closer to the shelf.

Focused as she was, Joy didn't notice him. She also didn't notice the mom with a stroller forming a temporary blockade. Lucas veered left. He kicked a wayward Lego toward the baby carriage's wheels, setting the contraption into lockdown.

His eyes were constantly scanning, anticipating. Finally, she was there. The Star Voyager toy was within Joy's arm's reach. And as he watched Joy score the toy, as he saw her triumph, her joy, her victory, he felt a surge of pride, of connection.

"Congratulations," he said.

"Thanks." She looked up at him, clutching the toy to her chest. "You're not going to fight me?"

"Why would I fight you when I wanted you to win? I've always wanted you to win."

"What about you?"

It was at that moment that the notification on his phone went off. It went off on hers too. She looked down and frowned. But then looked back at the toy in triumph.

"Some jerk outbid me in an online auction," she said. "But it's no matter. I got my toy."

"I'm a jerk."

"Yeah, I know."

"No." Lucas grinned, holding up his phone. "I won the auction."

"You won the auction? You were bidding against me?"

"Let me pay for the toy, make it a donation to the toy drive."

"I think you've paid enough." Her brow lifted as she looked at the final bid amount.

If only that were true. If he knew Joy, and he could say with certainty that he was the one who knew her best in the world, then Lucas would bet he had far more to pay to make up for his past mistakes.

"Thank you, Lucas," she said, her voice soft but firm. "But I've got this."

She was strong, she was independent, she was Joy. And Lucas loved her all the more for it.

He'd won the auction for Jamie. Joy had secured a

toy of her own for the drive. Now it was time to win the ultimate prize.

CHAPTER SEVEN

*J*oy stared out the car window, the street signs gliding by in a blur, yet her mind was miles away. The Star Voyager toy was packaged in a shopping bag tucked safely in her lap. But even as she clutched it, her heart was grasping for something else.

She couldn't shake off the image of Lucas back at the store, dashing through the chaos, moving people aside, basically clearing her path to the toy. He had been her knight, her savior, her champion. And now, as they drove in silence, she felt an ache in her chest, a longing that went beyond the joy of victory.

The car smelled faintly of his cologne, a scent that was all too familiar, all too intoxicating. It wrapped around her like a memory, pulling her back to a time when they were together, when they were one.

"You okay?" Lucas's voice broke through her reverie, concern etching his face.

"Just thinking about everything, you know? The toy drive, the kids, the way you... helped me back there."

Lucas smiled, a warm, genuine smile that reached his eyes. "I told you I would, didn't I? When have I ever let you down?"

It was right there on the tip of her tongue. She wanted to rail that he'd broken her heart that day he'd left to pursue advancement in the military. Joy was from a military town. She saw the sacrifice of military families every day. She would have stood by him, waited for him. Instead, he'd thought it best to sever ties.

She held her tongue. Because she wasn't ready to smash through the warm cocoon of care that had settled inside the car.

It had always been like this between her and Lucas. She'd never had to worry when she was with him. He'd always been there for her. Had always protected her. That's why his abandonment had hit so hard.

That display in the toy shop showed that he still

cared, still wanted to be there for her, still wanted to protect her. And yet, there was something more, something deeper, something that went beyond mere friendship.

It was like the universe was pulling them back together. It sounded crazy, but it was like fate wanted them to reconnect. The first store, the auction, the second toy. Destiny was calling them. But Joy wasn't ready to listen.

"I never stopped, you know," he said.

"Never stopped what?"

"Loving you."

The road stretched out before them. Lucas's hands were firm on the wheel. His profile was focused as he navigated the winding roads. There was a tightness to his jaw, a furrow in his brow that betrayed a deeper turmoil.

"When I took that job promotion, when I left you... it wasn't just about the opportunity or the career. It was about fear. Fear of commitment, fear of what we had, fear of what it meant."

The words were like daggers, cutting through the fabric of their past, exposing the raw truth. "You were afraid of us?"

"Yes, Joy. I was afraid. Afraid of losing myself, afraid of loving you too much, afraid of what it meant to be so utterly connected to someone. You were everything to me, and I was terrified of what that meant."

The car filled with his pain, his remorse, his longing. Joy felt it all. A tidal wave of emotion crashed over her, leaving her breathless, shattered.

"You were the one that got away, Joy," he continued, his voice raw. "You were the one I never stopped loving, the one I never stopped missing. And that boyfriend of yours, he better hang on tight to a prize like you. He better appreciate what he has."

Joy could hardly breathe. Lucas's words rang in her ears. The truth sank into her soul. She ached to reach out and take his hand, feel the familiar warmth, the comforting strength, the unparalleled love that was still there.

"Do you mind a detour? I have to grab the kids."

Joy's heart was still pounding at Lucas's admission. It skipped a beat as Lucas took a sudden turn off the main road. The car glided smoothly into a school parking lot, where children's laughter and playful chatter filled the air.

"Kids?" Her voice caught in her throat. The thought of meeting his children, his family, was overwhelming. It was a part of his life she hadn't prepared to face so soon.

"Is something wrong?" Lucas asked, his brows furrowed in concern.

"I... I'm just not ready to meet them," she stammered, her palms sweaty, her heart racing. "This is all so... so unexpected."

Lucas reached out and gently squeezed her hand. "It'll be fine, Joy. They'll love you."

Before she could respond, a joyful shout cut through the air. A little boy with tousled hair and sparkling eyes came running toward the car. "Uncle Lucas! Uncle Lucas!"

Lucas's face lit up, and he opened the door, sweeping the boy into a hug. "Hey, Jamie! How was school?"

"It was great. Look what I drew." The boy held up a colorful drawing, his face beaming with pride.

Nephew. That was the kid. Not his own. The relief that settled over Joy was swift. Her attention was soon drawn to the older girl who followed, a hint of preteen indifference in her eyes.

"Hi, Amber," Lucas greeted her warmly.

"Hey," Amber replied, rolling her eyes but smiling nonetheless.

Jamie. Amber. The connection clicked in Joy's mind. The realization was a jolt, and she looked down at the Star Voyager toy in her lap.

Jamie's eyes followed hers, and he gasped in delight. "Is that a Star Voyager? I hope Santa will bring me one."

Joy looked at Lucas. They had been fighting over a toy. For the same child. The irony, the serendipity, the sheer magic of the moment were not lost on her.

"Amber, Jamie, I want you to meet my oldest and dearest friend, Joy."

Joy could feel the warmth of his gaze, the promise in his eyes, the love that still lingered between them. She looked at the children, at the toy, at the man beside her, and she knew that this was no coincidence, no accident.

This was destiny.

She reached out and ruffled Jamie's hair, her voice soft, her eyes shining. "I think Santa might have a special surprise for you this year."

Jamie's eyes sparkled with delight. Amber's skepticism softened into a smile. Lucas's hand found hers, their fingers entwining, their hearts synching back up to beat as one.

CHAPTER EIGHT

The rich aroma of freshly brewed coffee wrapped around Lucas as he stepped into Sandy Perk. The familiar sights and sounds brought back a flood of memories from a time before deployments, heartache, and the loss that weighed on him. He chose a corner table that gave him a view of the door and settled into his seat. His fingers thrummed the top of the table as he waited in anticipation for his first date with Joy.

"Lucas," a warm voice called out, and he looked up to see the coffee shop owner, Aria Reynolds, beaming at him. "I haven't seen you in ages. How have you been?"

Lucas stood to greet her. "It's good to see you again, Aria."

"Look at you, all grown up." Aria wiped her hands on her apron before bringing him in for a hug. "I remember you and your brother coming in here all the time when my parents owned the place."

Lucas's heart clenched at the mention of his brother. The wound was still fresh. The pain was still raw. He looked down, a shadow crossing his face.

"I heard." Aria's touch gentled on his shoulder. "I'm sorry for your loss."

"He was the best brother anyone could ask for."

Brandon had passed away three years ago. Lost in a training operation on friendly soil. There had been no enemies in sight. No one to fight. Lucas and his family consoled themselves with the notion that Brandon had left this world the way he'd chosen to live in it, and that was in service to others.

"I'm sure he'd be proud of you, Lucas. You've become such a strong, brave man."

Lucas smiled, the ache in his heart easing a little. "I hope so."

"Chamomile and lavender tea on the house."

Lucas chuckled. Aria rarely allowed her patrons to actually place their own orders. When she was behind the bar, she took one look at them and made them the drink she thought they needed. There was no sense in arguing with her, so Lucas only nodded.

Aria patted his hand and bustled back behind the counter, leaving Lucas to his thoughts. He looked around the coffee shop, the memories of his brother mingling with the excitement of seeing Joy again. His heart ached for the past, but it also sang with hope for the future.

The door chimed, and he looked up. It wasn't Joy. It was double trouble: Holly and Felice. Their eyes met. He expected frowns. After all, he'd dumped their best friend and left her heartbroken. Instead, smiles broke across their faces.

"Lucas Jackson, is that you?" Holly rushed over to hug him.

"What are you doing here?" demanded Felice, but she smiled as she said the words.

"Does Joy know you're here?"

"I'm so glad you're back, so she'll finally stop dating these losers."

Lucas was used to the rapid-fire chatter between the Evergreen cousins. If Joy had been here, it would have been a triple threat.

"Losers?" asked Lucas.

The cousins looked at each other. Then they

SHANAE JOHNSON

looked out the window. Sly smiles lit their pretty faces.

"She's coming now."

"We need to make ourselves scarce."

But not before straightening Lucas's collar and brushing imagined lint off his shoulder. Felice went so far as to restyle his hair before Lucas brushed her hand away. And then they were out of the back door.

The front door chimed, and Lucas looked up. His breath caught in his throat as Joy walked in. She was radiant, her eyes wide and sparkling, her cheeks flushed with the cold of the season. Her dress clung to her curves, the soft fabric enhancing her natural grace. Her hair was pulled back, a few tendrils escaping to frame her face, and she looked absolutely stunning.

"Lucas." She grinned at him as she made her way over to him.

He was unable to take his eyes off her. Unable to speak for precious seconds. "You look beautiful, Joy."

She blushed, her eyes dropping for a moment before meeting his again. "Thank you. You look great too."

They sat, the world around them fading as they began to talk. Aria brought Lucas his steaming mug of herbal tea. She sat a mug of hot cocoa with extra whipped cream in front of Joy, though Joy hadn't placed an order.

Lucas listened intently, hanging on Joy's every word. He wanted to know everything that had happened since the day he left. And though he listened, he didn't catch much of what she said. Instead, he watched the way her lips moved, the way her eyes lit up.

While she sipped from her cup, Lucas shared stories of his own. After he'd been selected for Officer Candidate School, he was commissioned as a second lieutenant in the Army and relocated to a base in South Korea.

He told her about a hilarious night out with his unit at a local Korean restaurant. Eager to prove their mettle, they'd ordered a round of the spiciest dishes on the menu—only to regret their bravado minutes later. The locals were in stitches, watching them chug milk and fan their mouths.

Then there was that night out with fellow soldiers, which led to a series of escalating dares involving soju, the famous Korean alcoholic beverage. By the end of the evening, Lucas had been dared to dance to K-pop in the middle of the base's cafeteria—captured forever in a video that his buddies would never let him live down.

The best memories were the genuine friendships he'd formed with locals, especially a shop owner who'd served in the Korean military years before. Despite the language barrier, they shared a deep mutual respect and taught each other bits of their native tongues.

Joy licked the rim of her mug, snagging a remnant of hot cocoa. Lucas had to swallow in order to focus. He wanted nothing more than to be that porcelain cup.

"I was really nervous about this," Joy admitted, her fingers playing with the handle of the mug. "About seeing you and hanging out again."

"We're not hanging out, Joy. This is a date."

She grinned at him. More importantly, she did not contradict the label he put on this outing.

Lucas reached over, gently covering her hand with his. "I've missed you. More than I can say."

"I've missed you too, Lucas."

The soft hum of chatter, the gentle clinking of cups and saucers, the intoxicating aroma of fresh espresso all blended into a comforting backdrop. Aria and her baristas poured foamy lattes and cappuccinos with the precision of artisans. Each *clink* sounded like a cheerful note, punctuating the end of one sentence or the beginning of another in conversations that ebbed and flowed around them.

"I'm committed to being a guardian to Jamie and Amber. I'm committed to taking care of them, loving them, being there for them. I would like the opportunity, the chance, to recommit to you, too. Will you give us another try? Will you give our love another chance?"

CHAPTER NINE

*J*oy's apartment was filled with the festive rustle of wrapping paper and the sweet aroma of Holly's freshly baked Christmas cookies. Felice's soft humming of *Jingle Bells* gave a cheerful ambiance to the living room. Joy was seated at the small dining table, carefully wrapping gifts for the toy drive.

Joy felt a warm contentment as she looked at the carefully wrapped Star Voyager toy. Now that Jamie's Christmas wish had been granted by his uncle, she could surprise another deserving kid with the extra toy. The very thought of Lucas brought a gentle blush to her cheeks. It had been three days since they'd found their way back to each other amidst the battle of gift shopping.

He called every day. He didn't ask for an answer to the question he'd asked on their date. Joy had told him she needed time to think. But that wasn't true. She just needed time to catch her breath and slow her heart. They both knew that the organ belonged to him, and his to her.

"So, Joy," Holly began, her voice tinged with mischief, "are you going to tell us about your date with Lucas, or do we have to pry it out of you?"

Felice joined in, her eyes twinkling. "Yes, spill the beans. We want all the juicy details."

Joy tried to suppress a smile but failed. "It was... wonderful. We talked about everything. He was so open and honest with me."

Holly reached for a cookie. "Honest? That's a promising start. What did he say?"

Joy looked down at her hands, playing with the ribbon on the packaging. "He told me about his fears, about why he took the job and left me. He said he was scared of commitment but that now he's ready to be committed to me."

The cookie en route to Felice's mouth paused. "Wow, that's huge. How do you feel about that?"

"I feel hopeful. I mean, I still have my reservations, but something about the way he said it made me believe him. It's like the universe is giving us a second chance, and I don't want to let it slip away."

Holly reached over and squeezed Joy's hand. "That's beautiful, Joy. And scary too, I bet."

Joy shrugged. Not in nonchalance. It was a shrug of surrender. "I love him. It's always been that way. It always will."

"So you're going to give him another chance?"

Joy nodded. She could share this with her cousins. She wasn't ready to share it with Lucas. She still needed more time. For what, she wasn't sure.

"I think you're making the right decision," said Holly. "Love like yours doesn't come around often. You owe it to yourselves to give it another try."

"How are things going with you and choir boy?" Joy asked, needing to change the topic away from her love life.

Felice got a faraway look in her eyes, clearly thinking about her early Christmas present. The town choir had needed a strong baritone to complete the sound for the caroling concert, and one had arrived just in time.

"Mike is an amazing singer. When we duet, it's like there's no one else in the world besides us. But he's holding back in the relationship department. I'm not sure why."

"He's a fool if he doesn't snap you up," Holly insisted.

"Oh yeah? Well, what about you and Ryan?" said Felice.

Holly's older brother's best friend had recently come back into town. The two were working together on the holiday dinner for the children of the base. But Joy knew that things were spicing up in the kitchen.

"Shhhh," Holly hushed. "I know he's not here, but I'm so freaked that Garland will somehow find out. I don't want my big brother to know that I've had a crush on his best friend since we were kids."

"Oh, honey, he knows," said Felice. "Everybody knows."

Holly swatted at Felice, who ducked the blow. But not before swiping another cookie from the platter. Felice watched her cousins with a smile playing at her lips.

As they continued wrapping gifts, laughter and teasing filling the room, Joy felt a profound sense of gratitude. She knew she was embarking on a journey filled with uncertainty and challenges, but she also knew she had the love and support of her friends. And the love of Lucas.

With a happy sigh, she tied the final ribbon. She

was ready to embrace love once again, ready to face the future with Lucas by her side. She supposed she should probably tell him so.

The doorbell rang, a jarring chime that startled Joy.

Holly glanced at the clock. "I'll get it. Probably another delivery."

When Holly opened the door, Joy's heart skipped a beat. There was Lucas, standing on the entry with a bashful smile, holding a bag filled with more gifts.

"I thought you guys could use a hand," he said, stepping inside.

Joy's pulse quickened as their eyes met. Lucas looked more handsome than ever. The way he looked at her made her feel cherished and special.

"Well, perfect timing," said Holly, giving Felice a tug. "Felice and I were just saying we needed a coffee break."

Felice chimed in, a knowing sparkle in her eyes. "Yes, Lucas, why don't you stay and help Joy? I have to get to choir practice."

Before Joy could protest, her cousins had grabbed their coats and dashed out the door, leaving her alone with Lucas. The room suddenly felt warmer, the atmosphere charged with a connection that Joy could no longer deny.

"They're subtle," Lucas said, looking around at the colorful chaos.

"You don't have to help if you don't want to."

"I want to," he said, stepping closer to her. "Any reason to be around you."

His gaze slipped to her lips, then back up to her eyes. He held her there, imprisoned in his passionate gaze. She could have told him her decision right there. They could be wrapped up in each other instead of wrapping gifts.

Instead, she said, "Just grab some paper and follow my lead."

As they settled into wrapping the toys, their hands occasionally brushed against each other, sending a thrill down Joy's spine. The familiar banter between them flowed naturally. It was like old times. It was like no time had passed between them.

"I've got to pick up Jamie and Amber in a little bit," Lucas mentioned, carefully tying a ribbon.

"How are they doing?"

"They're adjusting. It's hard without their mom, but I'm doing my best to be there for them."

"You're an amazing uncle, Lucas. They're lucky to have you."

Lucas looked into her eyes, his expression tender.

"I'm the lucky one. And I'm lucky to have you back in my life, Joy."

She hadn't given him an answer. But she had never needed to say the words. It was obvious that the two of them belonged together. It was inevitable that they would end up back together.

And so when the wrapping paper fell from his hands, Joy replaced the decorative string with her own. She didn't need to tell him to embrace her. He simply did it. She didn't need to tilt her head back. He placed his index finger under her chin and did it for her. She didn't need to signal that she was open to receiving a kiss from him. He took it.

Because it was already his. She was already his. She had been born belonging to this man. He was simply coming to claim what was rightfully his.

Joy's arms snaked around Lucas's neck. Her hold on him tightened. Because just as she was his, he was hers.

Their kiss deepened as they staked that claim. The paths inside their hearts went even deeper this time. There could be nothing and no one that would ever tear up the roots they'd planted in each other's souls.

As they broke apart, Joy looked up at Lucas. Her eyes shone with love. She let herself relax. She knew in her heart that Lucas would not leave her again. Besides their love, he now had the responsibility of Jamie and Amber to keep him home.

The room, now filled with wrapped gifts and the lingering warmth of their embrace, seemed to glow with the promise of new beginnings. Love had found its way back to them, and Joy knew that this time, it was here to stay.

CHAPTER TEN

The smell of scrambled eggs and toasted bread filled the kitchen, a warm and inviting contrast to the chaos that had unfolded that morning. Lucas, in his newfound role as guardian to his niece and nephew, was facing a battle unlike any he'd encountered in his military career.

"Jamie, where are your pants? You can't go to school without pants."

As soon as the kid entered the house each day, his pants were off. Jamie would streak around in his underwear or watch television with his boney knees on display, or scratch his butt cheek, uncaring of who saw. Much like his father had done when they were younger.

"I don't know, Uncle Lucas." Jamie's voice came

from his bedroom, tinged with frustration. "I can't find them anywhere."

Amber, meanwhile, sat at the kitchen table, poking at her breakfast with a disdainful look. "I told you, Uncle Lucas, I'm a vegetarian now. I won't eat eggs."

"Since when, Amber?" Lucas glanced at the scrambled eggs, his brow furrowed. "You loved eggs last week."

"Things change," Amber said, her arms folded, her voice defiant.

The sizzle of the eggs in the pan, the clatter of Jamie searching for his pants, and Amber's determined refusal to eat her breakfast made Lucas's head spin. The scene was so far removed from the order and discipline of his military life that he felt a pang of helplessness.

Parenting was a battlefield. It was unpredictable, demanding, and required every ounce of patience and ingenuity he possessed.

"Okay, Amber, what will you eat then?"

"Cereal's fine," she replied, a triumphant smile playing on her lips.

"Found them," Jamie yelled, running into the kitchen with pants in hand but wearing two completely different shoes.

"Jamie, your shoes don't match." Lucas rubbed his temples as he stared at the mismatched footwear.

Jamie looked down and shrugged. "I like them this way."

Lucas felt like a general who had lost control of his troops. Each moment was a struggle, a negotiation, a battle of wills. This was just one battle. He could not, and would not, lose the war.

"All right, eat your cereal, Amber. Jamie, if you're happy with your shoes, I guess that's fine."

The remainder of the morning was a blur of packing lunches, finding books, and managing minor disputes. Finally, with both children dressed, fed, and ready, Lucas drove them to school.

As he pulled away from the curb and headed to the base, he allowed himself a small smile. This new role as guardian was undoubtedly the hardest job he'd ever had. It was also the most rewarding. In the midst of the battles and the strife, he knew he was building a connection with Jamie and Amber that was unbreakable. The love and trust of these children were the spoils, and he wouldn't give up, no matter how challenging the fight. He was committed to them, to Joy, to this new life.

The morning was crisp and cold as Lucas pulled into the parking lot of the military base. It was his first official day on the base. It was a new beginning, a new chapter, and one filled with possibilities. The distant sound of a drill sergeant barking orders was familiar as Lucas stepped out of his car.

Walking toward the main building, he felt a twinge of nostalgia. The uniformed personnel hustling about, the stringent military protocols, and the discipline in the air all reminded him of his earlier years of service.

Inside, Commander Mitchell's office was a study in military precision and decorum. The man himself, tall and stern with sharp, assessing eyes, was seated behind a desk cluttered with papers, maps, and a half-finished cup of black coffee with the Sandy Perk label wrapped around the Styrofoam.

"Ah, Captain Lucas, welcome," Commander Mitchell said, extending a firm hand. "I've been looking forward to meeting you."

"Thank you, sir," Lucas replied, meeting the commander's grip.

"Have a seat." Mitchell gestured, and Lucas complied.

The commander's eyes narrowed as he looked over Lucas's file. "Impressive record you have here, Captain. I must admit, though, looking at these credentials, the job we've planned for you seems... inadequate."

"What do you mean, sir?"

Commander Mitchell leaned back, eyeing Lucas thoughtfully. "I mean, Captain, that we might have something better suited for your skills. A promotion, if you will."

A promotion? This was unexpected, to say the least. Lucas's mind raced, a whirlwind of thoughts and possibilities. Until he remembered the last time a promotion was offered and taken. It had come at a cost he hadn't considered.

"I'm honored, sir, but may I ask what the position entails?"

"It's a leadership role, overseeing a critical division. More responsibility, more challenges, but I believe you're up for it."

Lucas's curiosity was piqued. His drive for advancement was also engaged. He thought of Joy and the promise of their rekindled love. Would this new role take him away from her and the family he was committed to supporting?

"I appreciate the offer, Commander, but I need to know what this means for my work-life balance. I have family responsibilities now."

Commander Mitchell nodded, understanding in

his eyes. "I respect that, Captain. We can make arrangements to ensure you have the time you need for your family. The job will be demanding, but it won't consume your life."

The words were a balm to Lucas's fears. He wasn't anywhere near finished with his military career. And the commander was right. The new duties he'd been assigned would not be a challenge. He knew he had to at least hear the man out.

And so Lucas leaned forward and did just that.

CHAPTER ELEVEN

The community center was alive with festive cheer, twinkling lights, and the excited chatter of volunteers. Joy found herself dressed as an elf, complete with pointy ears, a bright green tunic, and a red hat that seemed perpetually crooked. The scent of ginger and pine wafted through the air as she adjusted her hat, trying to take in the scene before her.

"Looking good, cuz," Holly called out, laughing, her own elfish attire shimmering with glitter. "You ready to spread some Christmas joy?"

"As ready as I'll ever be. I just hope I don't trip over these elf shoes."

Felice joined in the laughter. "Just think of the smiles on those kids' faces."

The room was filled with wrapped presents, each tagged with care and ready to be delivered to the children on the base and the families of soldiers. The gifts were more than just toys; they were symbols of love, support, and community.

"All right, elves," Joy called out. "Let's get these presents loaded up. We have a lot of families waiting for some Christmas magic."

The group sprang into action, working together to load the presents into vans, singing Christmas carols and sharing stories of holidays past. Joy felt a warm connection to these people, all working together to make the season brighter for others.

As they worked, she thought of Lucas and his family. Jamie and Amber, the little ones who had captured Lucas's heart, would be receiving gifts too. And Lucas, strong and caring, trying to fill the shoes of a parent. She saw the love in his eyes when he spoke of them.

"Joy, you ready to head out?" Felice asked, snapping her back to reality.

"Yes, let's do this," Joy replied, her excitement growing.

With the vans loaded, they set out, each taking different routes to spread cheer throughout the community.

Joy felt a tingling sense of elation as she maneu-
vered the van through the snow-dusted streets, its
back seat brimming with wrapped gifts adorned in
shiny paper and bows. With the candy-cane stripes
on her tights, she felt like Santa's most devoted
emissary.

As she pulled up to the first house, she could
already see kids peering eagerly through frosted
windows, their faces illuminated by the warm glow
of twinkling Christmas lights. The moment she
opened the van's door, a chorus of squeals erupted.

With each knock on a front door, she was met
with bright eyes and beaming smiles. The parents,
some in holiday sweaters, others in uniform just
home from a shift on the base, greeted her with a
warmth that melted any lingering chill from the
winter air.

"Thank you, Elf Joy," they'd say, their eyes often
brimming with unspoken emotion, a mixture of
relief and gratitude that their kids would have a
memorable Christmas. And every "you're welcome"
she offered was imbued with a humbling sense of
honor. This was the least she could do for families
who gave so much.

As she made her final stop for the day, the sun
dipped below the horizon, casting the world in the

soft, ethereal glow of twilight. She took a deep breath, the air tinged with the scents of burning firewood and home-cooked meals, and felt an overwhelming sense of contentment. This was the magic of Christmas, a magic made all the more special by the smiles she'd seen and the warmth she'd felt in the hearts of a grateful community.

Joy made sure her last stop was Lucas's house. Taking a deep breath, she grabbed Jamie's and Amber's presents and approached the door. She rang the bell, her heart in her throat, the sound of laughter and music drifting from inside. The door swung open, and there stood Lucas, his eyes widening in surprise and his face breaking into a warm smile.

"Joy? What are you doing here?"

"I'm here to deliver some Christmas magic," she said, holding up the presents.

His eyes softened, and she saw something deeper there, something that spoke of love and a shared future. She knew then that she was right where she was meant to be, with the man she loved and the community that was her forever home.

"Miss Joy, are you one of Santa's helpers?" Jamie squealed, bouncing on his toes, his eyes wide with anticipation.

"I sure am, and I have something for both of you." She handed Jamie his gift, and his face lit up like the Christmas tree in the corner of the room.

"Do you think it's a Star Voyager toy?" he asked, his voice filled with hope.

"Only one way to find out," Joy teased, her eyes twinkling. It was not. Joy had helped Lucas wrap the auctioned Star Voyager the other day. Joy had managed to get an accessory to the action figure. "But you're going to have to wait until Christmas morning to open it. Now, Amber, it's your turn."

Amber accepted the package with a quiet "Thank you," her demeanor more reserved, yet her eyes filled with gratitude.

Joy saw the depth of emotion in those young eyes, a wisdom beyond her years, born from loss and responsibility. She knew it wasn't the gift Amber wanted. She wished she could deliver that.

Then Amber's eyes suddenly widened, and she looked over her shoulder, her face lighting up. "Mommy?" she whispered.

Joy turned and saw a car pulling into the drive. The door opened, and a figure in a military uniform stepped out. It was their mother, returning from deployment, her face radiant with happiness and longing.

"Mommy!" Jamie and Amber screamed in unison, dropping their gifts and rushing out the door.

Joy stood frozen, tears welling in her eyes, witnessing this beautiful reunion. Lucas put a gentle hand on her shoulder, his touch grounding her.

The children flung themselves into their mother's arms, their cries of joy mingling with sobs of relief. Joy heard their mother's soothing words, felt the power of their embrace, and knew that this family was whole once again.

As she watched them, a sense of peace settled over her. Joy realized that love was the true magic of Christmas. It was in the laughter of children, the embrace of family, and the connection between two hearts destined to be together.

"I missed you so much, Amber," the mother whispered, her eyes filled with emotion as she kissed her daughter's forehead.

Then her eyes met Lucas's, and Joy saw a profound gratitude there. "Lucas, thank you," she said, her voice choked with emotion. "Thank you for everything you've done for my children. I don't know how I can ever repay you."

Lucas embraced her. "You're family, Ashley. There's nothing to repay."

Joy's heart ached with the beauty of the moment,

the love and sacrifice so evident in Lucas's actions. But then the mother's next words sent a chill through her.

"I've been permanently stationed on the base, Lucas," Ashley announced, her voice filled with relief and happiness. "And I heard about your new job promotion. That's incredible."

A job promotion?

The world outside seemed to tilt, the joyful sounds of the family reunion turning into a distant echo. Panic welled in Joy's chest as the realization hit her. Lucas was leaving. He was leaving her, just when she had started to believe in their future together.

Without a word, Joy turned and fled, her heart breaking with every step. She didn't hear Lucas calling her name or feel his hand reaching out to stop her. All she knew was the crushing weight of disappointment and fear.

Lucas was leaving. The man she had given her heart to, the man who had promised to be there for her, was leaving. And she was going to be left behind, her dreams shattered and her heart in pieces. The chaos of love had once again taken its toll, and Joy was left to pick up the fragments, wondering if she would ever trust again.

CHAPTER TWELVE

*L*ucas sprinted down the street after the van, the icy wind cutting through the cotton shirt he wore. But Joy was long gone. One moment they were celebrating the return of his sister-in-law, and the next, Joy was fleeing from him, a look of dejection in her eyes.

He didn't stop running. He didn't turn back to get his truck. Or a coat. Or boots. Nothing mattered but Joy.

He skidded to a halt outside her apartment. The panic within him drowned out all else. He banged on her door, calling her name, but there was no answer. The lights were off. A sinking feeling settled in his stomach.

Where could she be?

His mind raced as he dashed to Sandy Perk, the coffee shop where they had shared so many moments together. But the baristas there hadn't seen her. The warm aroma of freshly brewed coffee turned bitter in his nose as he turned on his heel and headed back out the door.

By the time he got to the community center, his breath was visible in the cold air. His teeth chattered, but it was nothing in comparison to the whirlwind of confusion and fear going on inside his mind.

Finally, he found himself at the church. He was drawn there by the ringing sound of Christmas carols. The choir practice was in full swing singing *Joy to the World*. But Joy was nowhere to be found inside.

Felice stood at the helm, directing the boisterous voices. Her gaze was on one singer in particular. Lucas recognized Mike Harrington standing off to the side. Or rather, he recognized Mike's voice first. The baritone had been the best singer in the high school chorus.

Lucas waited until the group took a break. Then he approached Joy's cousin. "Felice, have you seen Joy?"

"She was out delivering presents for the toy

drive." Felice's gaze narrowed on Lucas in suspicion. "What's gone wrong?"

"I don't know what went wrong. She delivered Jamie and Amber's gifts. Then she just took off after my sister-in-law returned home."

Felice's face turned thoughtful, and she said, "You know, Joy mentioned that one of the reasons she agreed to give you another chance was because of your guardianship of the kids. Maybe your sister-in-law returning home rattled her."

"I'm staying," Lucas insisted, his voice rising. "I even accepted a promotion on the base. I hadn't told anyone, but my sister-in-law knew."

Realization dawned on both their faces. Lucas felt a chill that had nothing to do with the cold weather. The promotion.

"Joy overheard," he whispered. "She overheard Ashley talking about the promotion."

That was when she took off. Lucas had planned to tell her about the promotion. The gift-giving hadn't seemed like the best moment.

"She must have freaked out when she heard," Felice was saying. "When you left that first time, it hit her really hard, Lucas. I don't think she's ever opened her heart up to another guy. In fact, she's only dated losers. If any of them showed any initiative, she dumped them the next day."

All because of him. All because he'd once chosen his career over her. It had been the worst mistake in his life. One he'd learned from.

Lucas had made certain that the job promotion Commander Mitchell offered him came with permanent roots on the base. There was no way he could leave Joy again, even if it meant career advancement. The job was local, but Joy didn't know that. She thought he was going to leave her again.

Lucas's heart sank, the realization hitting him like a punch to the gut. How could he have let this happen? How could he have allowed Joy to misunderstand?

The sweet sound of the choir was a haunting backdrop to the chaos of his emotions. The scent of candle wax and the soft rustling of sheet music were distant and unimportant as he stood there, feeling lost and broken.

"I have to find her," he said. "I have to show her that I'm not leaving her again."

Felice placed a reassuring hand on his shoulder, her eyes filled with sympathy. "Go, find her, Lucas. Show her what's in your heart. Show her that your heart is hers."

It was hers. His heart had only ever belonged to Joy. The thought of her was what got him through the roughest days during his deployments. Lucas loved his country, but she was the main reason he fought—to keep her safe.

He nodded at Felice, his resolve hardening. Lucas headed out into the cold night, the weight of his mistake heavy on his shoulders. He would find Joy, no matter what it took. He would show her that his love was true, that he was committed to her, now and forever.

CHAPTER THIRTEEN

*C*hristmas morning dawned with a gray chill. Inside Joy's heart, the weather felt even colder. Betrayal and confusion weighed heavily on her as she left her bedroom, the smell of pine from the Christmas tree mingling with the bitter-sweet taste of loss.

Lucas had accepted a promotion. He was leaving, just when she had started to believe in their future together.

Her feet moved mechanically, leading her to the tree adorned with twinkling lights. The reflection in the ornaments resembled a distorted image of her conflicted emotions. A glimmer caught her eye—a mysterious letter sat on the floor in front of her front door at the mail slot.

It was Christmas. There was no mail delivery.

Joy went over to the envelope. On the front, in bold print, read "From Santa." The print might have been bolded Sharpie, but Joy recognized it. This was Lucas's handwriting.

Did she dare open it? Could she stand to hear any of what he might have to say to her? Already, her body was missing his warmth. Her cheek missed that place right in the middle of his shoulder that seemed curved to fit the size of her head. Her lower back missed the weight of his hand. Her ears missed the sound of his voice.

With all the missing going on, Joy was overruled. Her fingers tore through the envelope. Her eyes scanned the words even as her brain rejected the idea of any hope for a future with Lucas.

"Follow the lights to find your Christmas wish," the note read.

Joy yanked the door open. He wasn't there. Instead, there was a trail of tiny lights.

She stared for a moment. A cold, wintry wind whipped around her pajama bottoms as she stood in the open doorway. Again, her body made the decision for her as she whirled on her feet to race back into her bedroom. Once properly attired, she dashed out the door to follow the light trail.

Joy couldn't help the mixture of hope and trepidation building within her. The cold air bit at her cheeks as the path guided her through the snow. The soft glow of the lights was a gentle guide. The ornaments hanging along the way were a silent promise.

A promise of what, though? Lucas was leaving. She'd heard it confirmed by his sister-in-law. She couldn't stand to let that happen again. Still, her feet kept propelling her forward.

Finally, she arrived at a clearing. The sight took her breath away. Lucas had transformed the place into a magical Christmas scene, complete with a festive breakfast spread under a canopy of twinkling lights. The aroma of gingerbread and fresh pastries filled the air, making Joy wonder if Holly had a hand in this. The Christmas carols playing from somewhere overhead let her know that Felice had definitely participated in creating this scene.

"Joy." The way he said her name was like the answer to a prayer.

How could he say her name like that, so soft and filled with emotion, when he was planning on leaving her again? He *was* planning on leaving her again, wasn't he? The look in his eyes gave Joy pause. Lucas didn't look like a man preparing to break up. He looked like a man ready to put up a fight.

"The first thing I need you to know is that I'm not leaving."

It took Joy a few times of rewinding the words in her head to be sure she heard him. As though he sensed her doubts, Lucas strode to her. He took her hands in his, squeezing his warmth into them, and repeated the words.

"I'm not leaving."

It was all Joy needed to hear. Everything he said after that was entirely inconsequential. Still, some of it penetrated.

"That wasn't the way I wanted you to hear about the promotion. I had every plan to tell you about it. I almost didn't take it when it was first offered because I knew I could never be parted from you again. But then the commander said it was a position here on the base, one that would challenge me and allow me to grow."

Tears welled in Joy's eyes as she looked at him. Lucas and his love and commitment radiated from every pore of his being. The breakfast he'd prepared, the setting, the lights, all were a testament to his feelings for her.

"I'm not leaving you. How could I? Every day with you is Christmas for me, and I want to make that a reality."

The joy and relief that flooded her were indescribable. The weight lifted, and her heart soared. She threw herself into his arms, the cold forgotten. Their lips met in a kiss that sealed their promise.

The world around them faded away, the twinkling lights a soft embrace, the smell of snow and pine a gentle reminder of the season. They sat down at the breakfast Lucas had prepared, laughter and love filling the air, the fear and misunderstanding a thing of the past.

Joy realized with a heart full of love that she had indeed found her Christmas wish. Lucas was her forever, her always, her Christmas every day. And as they sat there, hand in hand, she knew that nothing could ever take that away.

CHAPTER FOURTEEN

*T*he Jackson living room was a symphony of Christmas—the twinkling of tree lights reflecting off glass ornaments, the sweet and spiced aroma of cookies wafting from the kitchen, and the quiet rustle of tissue paper accompanying the quiet gasps of wonder. Lucas sat on the couch. Joy's hand was firmly entwined with his. Inside his chest crept a warmth that had nothing to do with the fireplace crackling in the corner.

"Okay, Jamie, Amber, you can start," he announced, struggling to contain his own excitement.

Jamie tore through the gifts with gusto. The kid was a whirlwind of kinetic energy, shredding paper and unearthing gifts like a pint-sized hurricane. Yet what caught Lucas's attention wasn't just the boy's enthusiasm, but the gratitude that followed each unwrapping, regardless of the gift. From socks and books to small gadgets, Jamie's excitement remained constant.

As the mound of torn wrapping paper grew, Lucas felt his heart drumming in his chest. Hidden amongst the rubble was the pièce de résistance, the much-coveted Star Voyager toy. His palms were a bit sweaty as Jamie reached for the final box—a nondescript, rectangular package.

Lucas noted that Amber wasn't unwrapping any of her gifts. Instead, she watched her brother as she sat next to her mother. A small smile played at her normally frowning mouth as her gaze went from her mom to her brother.

Reaching for one of the presents, Lucas handed it to the preteen.

Amber looked at the elegantly wrapped box in front of her, then slowly lifted her gaze to her mother's eyes. "You know, sometimes the best gifts aren't the ones wrapped in shiny paper and bows. Sometimes they can't be held but can only be felt. I have the only gift I've wanted all year right here."

Her mother's eyes overflowed this time, and she embraced her daughter, enveloping her in a hug so warm and enveloping, it spread throughout the room.

Lucas felt Joy's fingers tighten around his. He looked down to find her eyes shimmering.

"Thank you, Santa," Amber said softly, her gaze meeting Joy's.

Lucas could've offered the same sentiment. Santa's helper, who sat beside him, had given him the only gift in the world he wanted.

"The Star Voyager!" Jamie finally erupted.

As he clutched the toy, Lucas could practically see the fantasies taking flight in Jamie's mind— adventures among the stars, battles against cosmic foes, voyages to distant galaxies. For a child, a toy could be a vessel to unexplored universes, and Lucas felt honored to hand him the keys to such a journey.

"Thank you, thank you, thank you," Jamie couldn't stop repeating, his little arms squeezing Lucas and Joy in a bear hug that left both adults breathless but beaming.

"That was, Santa, buddy."

"But you helped," said Jamie. "I know you did."

As Lucas returned the hug, he realized how completely entangled his happiness was with this small tribe of his. And at the core of it, sitting side by side with him, was Joy. She was the compass that guided him, the star that navigated him back home no matter how far he strayed.

He leaned down and kissed her, tasting the sweet promise of endless tomorrows on her lips. It was a soft, lingering kiss, an exclamation mark on the swirling emotions of the day. As they pulled apart, he realized that this was it—his once fragmented world was now a completed jigsaw puzzle, each piece in its rightful place.

Jamie and Amber chattered excitedly. Their mother gently wiped her tears. Joy leaned into Lucas as if she belonged nowhere else, and he knew. Lucas knew he had found his ultimate Christmas miracle. A family united, a love reignited, and a future so bright it made the twinkling Christmas lights pale in comparison.

Don't miss the next book in the Honor Valley Holiday series!

Two souls find warmth in harmony, but will a fading melody steal their chance at love?

. . .

Felice Evergreen loves nothing more than directing the town's choir for the annual Christmas carol concert. Unfortunately, what's missing from the ensemble is a soulful baritone. When Felice happens upon a man with a rich and resonant voice, her heart urges her to snag Mike for a duet.

Mike Harrington loves music; making it as well as singing songs. But a blast during his last deployment has left him struggling with progressive sensorineural hearing loss. When he returns to his small town, he's surprised when the church choir director asks him to join the group. As Mike and Felice grow closer, their voices blend in perfect harmony, and he starts to hear a different tune—a love song that he's afraid might end too soon.

Can love ring loud and clear or will silence grow between them? Find out in this holiday romance that weaves together the healing of a wounded hero, the determination of a small town heroine, the magic of music, and the spirit of the holidays.

· · ·

Love on a Silent Night is a part of the Honor Valley Holiday romances; a heartwarming, small town, military romance series that explores the power of love, growth, and healing set during the most magical time of the year! These stories are short and sweet -the perfect length for an afternoon pick me up or an evening escape before bedtime!

SHANAE JOHNSON

Love on a
Silent Night

HONOR VALLEY HOLIDAYS

CHAPTER ONE

*M*ike Harrington stared out the frosted car window as it pulled into the snow-draped driveway of his childhood home in Honor Valley. The familiar white two-story house, festooned with twinkling Christmas lights, should have been a comfort to him. But as he gazed at the snowy scene, Mike couldn't shake the feeling that he was a stranger in a land he'd once known intimately.

"Here we are, son," George Harrington said, his voice booming from the front seat of the car. "Home sweet home."

"Thanks, Dad." Mike's voice was low and subdued, betraying none of the enthusiasm his father radiated.

Marianne Harrington turned in her seat to face

her son, her brown eyes bright with excitement. "You're going to love what we've done with the Christmas tree this year, honey. I'm just sorry you didn't get to decorate with us. We didn't expect you..."

And there she trailed off. They hadn't expected him home before the holidays. But with his injury, he had been medically discharged from the military.

"I can't wait to see it, Mom." Mike appreciated their efforts, but it didn't lessen the feeling of disconnect gnawing at him like a persistent ache. When he looked up, he saw his mother's lips moving again. "I'm sorry, Mom. What did you say?"

Marianne's cheerful smile faltered. She shared a quick glance with her husband before raising her voice. "Your old friends will be so glad to see you, too. I bet they'll be stopping by any minute."

"Can't wait," Mike said flatly, unbuckling his seatbelt and stepping out of the car.

The icy air hit him like a slap in the face, but he barely registered it. He trudged through the snow toward the front door, leaving behind fresh footprints. He'd grown up in this small town, surrounded by people who loved and supported him, but now it seemed more like a foreign country than the place that had been his home base.

"Come on, let's go inside," Marianne urged, slipping her arm through his. "I made your favorite cookies, and we can have some hot cocoa by the fire."

"Not just yet, Mom. I think I'm going to take a walk first. Stretch my legs."

His parents exchanged worried glances, but in the end, they nodded their consent. Not that he needed their permission to walk across the street or into town. He was twenty-six years old and had left home shortly after walking across the stage to receive his high school diploma.

Mike strolled down Honor Valley's Main Street, where the snow crunched beneath his boots and the air was crisp with winter's chill. Storefronts sparkled with twinkling lights and festive window displays. The scent of cinnamon and pine mingled with the faint echo of carolers in the distance.

But when he looked over his shoulder, he saw that the carolers were in fact just across the street. Still, their voices sounded as though they were at the far end of Main Street. It sounded as though one of them was calling his name as part of the song, but he knew that couldn't be right.

Mike turned away and bumped into a man waving his hands in front of Mike's face.

"Yo, Harrington!"

A firm hand gripped his shoulder as he turned around. Mike turned with his fist raised, ready to strike down the assailant. It wasn't any enemy. It was a friend.

Mike had gone to school with Scott Ream. The two had ridden the bus together and played Magic the Gathering in the library. The cheerful grin on Scott's face faltered when he saw Mike's fist.

"Sorry, man, I didn't hear you," Mike apologized, his cheeks flushing as he lowered his arm.

"It was my fault." Scott held up his hands as he backed away. "Well, uh, good seeing you, man. Catch you later."

With that, he strode off, leaving Mike feeling even more disconnected than before. The walk down memory lane had darkened, and Mike decided to head home before he saw anyone else he'd known from before.

Inside the house, the fire was crackling, though Mike didn't hear the sound clearly. Steam rose from the kettle on the stove. Mike only barely heard the whistling, but he smelled the rich aroma of hot chocolate as his mom tipped the teapot over and poured out three mugs.

Mike's hearing went in and out, like someone

messing with the dial on the radio. As he sat in front of the Christmas tree, his mother's humming along to Christmas tunes went in and out too. His father turned on a football game, and though Mike saw the numbers on the volume increase as George pointed the remote at the television, he only barely caught what the announcer was saying about the game.

"…bakery that opened up by the park?" His mother leaned forward, eager for a response.

"Sorry, what?" Mike replied, his brow furrowing in confusion.

Marianne repeated her question about the new bakery opening in town, raising her voice to a level that made both son and father wince. When she realized what she was doing, she bowed her head, her shoulders sagging slightly in disappointment.

"Maybe you can go with us this week," George chimed in. "They have the best cinnamon rolls in town."

"Sure," Mike agreed, though he doubted whether he'd be able to fully enjoy the outing.

"Look what we got for you, Mike." Marianne handed him a box wrapped in shiny red paper. "We thought these might help you out."

Mike tore off the wrapping to reveal a new pair of noise-canceling headphones. It wasn't the right direction he was aiming for his hearing to go. Mike wanted to hear things. He didn't want to cancel the noise out.

"Thank you, Mom, Dad." He wanted to convey just how much their efforts to make him comfortable meant to him. Yet as he slipped on the headphones, the silence that enveloped him only served to amplify his feelings of isolation and loneliness.

Retreating to his room after dinner, Mike sought refuge in the familiar comfort of music. The headphones were good for that. They canceled out the rest of the world and made the music sound crisp and clear in his failing ears. With each song he played, he tried to drown out the lingering sense of silence that clung to him like a shadow.

As the night wore on, he promised himself he'd try harder tomorrow—to reconnect, to be present, to find his way back to the people who mattered most. For now, though, he could only allow the comforting embrace of his old favorite tunes to lull him to sleep, dreaming of simpler times when the laughter of loved ones rang clear and true in his ears.

CHAPTER TWO

*F*elice Evergreen stood amidst the church choir's practice room, her wavy blonde hair cascading down her shoulders as she raised her arms in time with the music. Her bright blue eyes sparkled with passion and enthusiasm as she led the rehearsal for the annual Christmas carol event. The choir members' voices harmonized beautifully under her guidance, filling the room with festive cheer.

"All right, everyone, let's take it from the top again."

Felice was determined to make this year's performance unforgettable. She knew that dedication and hard work would be key. Her upbeat personality, coupled with her genuine love for music, made her the ideal choir leader.

"Hey, sis, great job today."

Felice grinned at her lanky younger brother as he approached during a break in the practice session. David's mop of curly blond hair bounced as he walked, his face bearing an enthusiastic grin. As a member of the choir, he shared his sister's love for music and passion for perfection.

"Thanks, Navidad." Felice returned his smile.

"Don't call me that," he groaned.

To say that their parents were Christmas enthusiasts was putting it mildly. The Evergreens owned the Christmas tree farm and a year-round Christmas store in Honor Valley. And all year round, business was booming. It made perfect sense to Felice that people would want a little Christmas cheer on a rainy spring day, or in the swelling heat of summer, or fall, and come into the shop in anticipation of the greatest season of the year.

"We're getting closer to nailing it," Felice said. "I just wish we could find a strong male voice to complete our performance."

"Well, if you wait another year, maybe my voice will deepen enough to fit the bill." David chuckled, adjusting his glasses.

His joke prompted laughter between the siblings. David was well out of puberty. He might be four years younger than Felice, having just turned eighteen. But their relationship was a close-knit one full of sibling secrets and lots of songs.

"Until then, I guess I'll have to keep searching," Felice sighed, glancing over at David's latest technological creation—a small robotic device that moved gracefully across the floor. It was no secret that her brother was a genius when it came to technology and making gadgets. "Think you could make me a robot or synthetic voice that could sing beautiful harmonies?"

"Give me a couple of months to perfect it." David's eyes lit up at the challenge. "I'm sure I could come up with something."

"I don't have months. Christmas is just a couple of weeks away."

Felice's thoughts drifted toward the mistletoe hanging over the doorway as they left the practice room together. A strong male voice wasn't the only thing she wished for for Christmas. She was hoping Santa would finally make good on the wish she'd been writing on her list since she was a teenager. Felice wanted to meet her true love and share a kiss under the mistletoe.

But she'd have to make time for love later. Right now, the break was over and choir practice was resuming. They had to get these songs right to help spread the Christmas cheer through the valley.

Felice's friend on the military base had told her that budget cuts had hit the families there hard. The first stop on the choir's homespun tour would be to bring some vocal Christmas spirit to the children on the base, making it even more important that they nail these carols.

The flickering glow of the setting sun filled the church's practice room, casting a warm, golden light on the rows of chairs and music stands that were meticulously arranged for the choir members. Felice tapped her baton against the edge of the stand.

"All right, everyone," she began, her voice melodious and encouraging. "Let's give it our all in this one."

As she raised her baton, the choir members took their positions, holding their sheet music with anticipation. With a flourish, Felice signaled for the music to begin, and the room was filled with the harmonious voices of her dedicated singers.

"Beautiful, simply beautiful," Felice exclaimed with genuine delight as the choir executed each note to perfection. She felt the energy in the room, the passion for music that each member shared, and it only fueled her own enthusiasm.

"Okay, let's move on to 'O Holy Night,'" she instructed, her eyes scanning the room as she mentally noted any areas for improvement. "Remember to really emphasize the crescendo in the chorus."

The familiar melody of 'O Holy Night' filled the air. The choir's voices swelled in unison as they reached the powerful climax of the song. Pride filled Felice's heart as she conducted them through the final notes. It wasn't perfect, but it was very, very good.

Unfortunately, even two verys weren't good enough for Felice. She knew exactly the tenor she needed to make the choir perfect. She'd just have to put out more feelers for a strong male voice at this Sunday's service.

Felice didn't let on that anything was missing from the performance. Only her brother, able to read her facial expressions from the time she'd cradled him in her arms, could tell. The choir members beamed at Felice's praise, their cheeks flushed with a mix of exertion and excitement. As they chatted among themselves, Felice made her way through the rows of chairs, stopping to offer feedback and encouragement to each singer.

"Mary, your soprano voice is truly angelic," she said to a middle-aged woman with silver-streaked hair. "Just remember to keep your chin up during those high notes. It'll help you project even more beautifully."

"Thank you, Felice," Mary replied, her eyes shining with gratitude. "I'll definitely work on that."

The choir members gathered their belongings and said their goodbyes. Felice was the last one left standing in the practice room. It really had been a good practice tonight. A very, very good one.

As she stood there, surrounded by the now empty rows of chairs and music stands, Felice glanced up at the mistletoe hanging overhead. Its vibrant green leaves and delicate white berries seemed to hold a promise just within reach.

"Come on, Fe," David called from down the hall. "Mom's hot chocolate will be cold if you take any longer."

With a hopeful heart, she offered up a silent wish as she stood beneath its boughs, trusting that this year, her Christmas dreams might finally come true.

And as her brother's laughter filled the air, she knew that even if her wish remained unfulfilled, she was already blessed with the love of her family and friends, and that was a gift worth cherishing.

CHAPTER THREE

"Look, Santa's over there!" A child's voice rang out, pulling Mike's attention to a makeshift Christmas village set up near the boardwalk.

"Santa will grant all my wishes this year," the little boy continued. "Including getting me a Star Voyager toy."

"There is no Santa," said a little girl a few inches taller than him with the same eyes. "If there was, then Mom would come home for Christmas instead of being deployed."

Mike clenched his jaw, frustrated that such innocence could exist in a world where he knew miracles didn't happen—at least not for people like him. His own belief in Santa and the magic of Christmas had long since faded, replaced by the harsh truth of the suffering he'd seen in third world countries during his time as a military medic.

Despite his bitterness toward the holiday season, one aspect of Christmas still held a special place in Mike's heart: the carols. He couldn't help but hum along to the familiar melodies playing from speakers strategically placed around the festive scene. With the songs blaring through the loud sound system, he heard each joy-filled carol perfectly.

Mike strolled along the beach as the salty breeze brushed against his face. It was far from the combat zones he'd known, far from the sound of gunfire and echoing explosions. Now the world around him was quiet, a stark contrast to the chaos he was used to. The irony wasn't lost on him.

His worn boots crunched into the icy sand, a sensation he felt more than heard. It resonated up through the soles of his boots, vibrating subtly into his bones. It was like a silent symphony only he could understand, a poignant reminder of his encroaching condition—progressive sensorineural hearing loss.

Mike knew how to administer first aid, including wound care, fracture stabilization, and CPR, among other life-saving techniques. But the workings of the inner ear were beyond his skill set.

The roar of the ocean was a distant, muffled sound, almost like a dream echoing from afar. He closed his eyes, trying to soak in the sound. The rhythmic ebb and flow of the waves were therapeutic, their once comforting whispers now slipping further away from him with each passing day.

Once, he could distinguish the subtlest notes of nature's orchestra—the distinctive caw of gulls, the rustling of wind through coastal grasses, even the delicate patter of snowflakes on the sand. Now those sounds were fading, drowned out in a sea of encroaching silence. He walked the line where the waters met the sand, where the sound met the silence. And all he could do was cherish the auditory fragments of the world he still held on to before they, too, slipped away.

Far away from the sound system of the town square, the rhythm of the crashing waves offered a sense of peace, and he found himself humming a familiar Christmas tune. The waves provided a steady beat, helping him keep time with the music. As he walked closer to the water, he thought he heard a faint voice singing along with him. He frowned, unsure if it was a trick of his impaired hearing or if someone was actually there. He scanned the shoreline, wondering who else would be out here on this chilly day.

That's when he saw her—a woman with long, curly hair cascading down her back, her bright smile illuminating the overcast sky. She walked toward him, her voice sweet and genuine. And clear as a bell.

Their eyes met, and for a moment, time seemed to stand still. They both stopped singing, their smiles widening as they took in each other's presence. It was a classic "meet cute" moment, straight out of a Hallmark movie.

"Hi," she called out, her voice carrying over the sound of the waves. "I'm Felice. I couldn't help but join in when I heard you singing. You have a beautiful voice. So resonant and… deep."

"Uh, thanks," Mike replied, his cheeks flushing in the brisk cold. "I didn't think anyone else would be out here."

"I come here to clear my head sometimes. There's something about the sound of water that just makes everything seem... smaller, you know?"

Mike didn't answer. He'd just cursed a world where miracles didn't happen. Looking at Felice and her smiling face and her voice that he heard so clearly, it seemed that maybe there was still some magic left in this world after all.

"Are you new in town?" she asked. "I don't think I've seen you around before."

"Used to live here, actually," Mike admitted. "Just got back recently."

"From college?"

"From overseas," Mike revealed, meeting her gaze with a mix of vulnerability and pride. "I was in the military. I'm Mike."

"Thank you for your service, Mike," Felice said, appraising him anew. "And welcome home."

She bit her lip, seeming to hesitate, as though she had to ask him something delicate. Mike stepped closer, not wanting to miss a word she said. Whatever it was, the answer would be yes.

"Mike, I don't suppose you'd be interested in joining the town choir?"

Mike stepped back, caught off guard by the ask.

"You have a lovely voice, exactly what I need. I mean exactly what we—the choir—need. We could really use a voice like yours."

Mike hesitated, torn between his love for singing and the fear of exposing his hearing loss to others. But as he looked into Felice's inviting eyes, something deep within him whispered that maybe, just maybe, this was his chance to regain a sense of belonging and purpose.

"The choir? I'm not sure it's the right fit for me."

"Why not? You clearly love Christmas carols, and you have an amazing voice."

"It's just…" Mike liked how Felice looked at him, assuming nothing was wrong. He wanted to keep her looking at him that way. He also wanted to sing with her again. But just her. "It's just that I might not be able to keep up with a group."

"Is that all?" Felice asked, her tone light and encouraging. "Our choir is filled with people from all walks of life, each bringing their own unique talents and challenges. It's about coming together and creating something beautiful, not being perfect."

She took a step closer, placing a comforting hand on his arm. "Besides, I'll be right there with you. If you ever need help keeping up, just let me know."

Mike stared into her eyes, feeling a warmth spread from his toes, up through his gloved fingers, and straight into his chest.

"So what do you say? Will you give it a try?"

CHAPTER FOUR

"All right, everyone." Felice clapped her hands to gather attention. "Let's talk music selection."

It was fifteen minutes after choir practice was supposed to start. The last of the members had come into the door, bringing the evening chill with them. Unfortunately, Mike was nowhere in sight.

Felice refused to let that dampen her spirits, but it was a losing battle. His voice would be perfect for the group. His smile would be just the thing to brighten up a chilly night.

"Felice, who will do the male vocals?" one choir member asked, knitting her brows in concern. "We can't have an unforgettable performance without a strong male voice."

Before Felice could reply, the heavy wooden doors at the entrance creaked open, and Mike stepped into the room. A hush fell over the choir, leaving only the faint rustle of the music pages and the distant hum of the heater.

"There's our answer." Felice beamed at the man in question.

She'd forgotten how tall Mike was. Those broad shoulders took up much of the room. There was a look of hesitancy and discomfort on his face as he peered around at all of the eyes on him. Despite his withdrawn demeanor, Felice knew he possessed a deep, resonant singing voice that would be perfect for their performance.

"Welcome, Mike," Felice called out, her warm smile inviting him into the space.

Mike offered a tentative smile in return. As he approached the choir, Felice's cheeks flushed with a rosy hue, her heart fluttering like a hummingbird. She took a deep breath to get her emotions under control, which didn't do much good. Stepping forward, she extended a welcoming hand. When Mike's fingers wrapped around hers, Felice heard jingle bells in her head.

"Mike, I'd like you to meet the choir members." She gestured to the group, who offered friendly smiles and nods. "Everyone, this is Mike. He'll be joining us as our male vocalist."

"Welcome, Mike," chorused the members.

"Thanks," Mike replied, his eyes meeting Felice's for a brief moment before he turned to face the choir. There was something in that glance that made Felice's pulse quicken.

"Hey, Fe," David whispered, nudging her elbow, "you better watch out or your crush on our new star will be as obvious as Santa's red suit."

"Shush," Felice hissed, swatting her brother on the arm.

Despite her mock annoyance, she couldn't deny the truth in David's words. Mike had captivated her from the moment they met. Now with him standing among the choir, his presence only seemed to intensify her feelings.

"All right, everyone," Felice announced, regaining her composure. "Let's start with 'Silent Night,' and remember to focus on your harmonies."

As the choir began to sing, Felice heard Mike's resonant voice weaving through the melody, adding depth and richness to the familiar carol. Each note floated through the air, wrapping around her like a warm embrace.

"Wow, Fe," David whispered as the song ended, a

grin playing on his lips. "If your face gets any pinker, we might not need Rudolph to guide our sleigh tonight."

"Enough, David," Felice said with a roll of her eyes.

She stole another glance at Mike. The growing attraction between them was undeniable. Felice had the feeling she might get her Christmas wish after all.

As the choir launched into 'O Come, All Ye Faithful,' Felice kept a careful ear on Mike. His voice rang out, beautiful and strong, but she noticed he struggled to stay in sync with the other voices. During the break, Felice made her way over to him.

He looked up at her approach. He stood a little taller, his back a little straighter. But there was concern on his face. Had he realized he was just slightly off the beat?

"Mike, you're doing great," she assured him, offering an encouraging smile.

"Are you sure? I haven't sung with others in a while. I thought I might be out of tune."

"No, not at all. Your voice is perfect. But I can see you're having some trouble keeping up."

The grin that had begun to blossom on his handsome face fell like a snowball turned to ice.

"How about I sing with you for a bit? We'll find the beat together."

Mike nodded, his eyes revealing a mix of gratitude and embarrassment. "I appreciate it."

As the choir began anew, Felice stood beside Mike and sang. Her soprano blended perfectly with his baritone. She kept sneaking glances at him and noticed he did the same. Felice's excuse was to make sure he was on the beat. She assumed he watched her for the same reason. In the end, it was clear that they sang to each other.

Mike's tense posture gradually relaxed. His shoulders loosened as he began to find his place within the song. They stood close enough that she felt the warmth of his breath against her cheek. It sent a pleasant shiver down her spine. By the time the song was over, Felice realized that theirs were the only two voices carrying any of the notes. When the last verse rang out, she and Mike ended to the sound of raucous applause.

"That was perfect," she said to Mike.

"Thanks to you."

The moment hung between them like a delicate snowflake. But before either could say anything more, the church bells chimed, signaling the end of their practice.

"Amazing job, everyone," Felice said, her voice brimming with genuine appreciation. Tonight's choir practice hadn't been good; it had been great. "We are going to sound incredible at the performance."

"Thanks to you and Mike, I think we have a real shot at making this year's concert unforgettable," one choir member chimed in, earning nods of agreement from the others.

"Here, here!" David declared, throwing an arm around Felice's shoulders. "Our fearless leader has done it again."

"Stop," she laughed, lightly pushing her brother away.

But as her eyes met Mike's once more, she couldn't deny the spark that seemed to crackle between them like a fire on Christmas Eve. As everyone went up to Mike to congratulate him, Felice wondered if this Christmas would bring not only a memorable performance but perhaps something even more magical, like that kiss under the mistletoe from the man of her dreams.

CHAPTER FIVE

"*D*id you know that 'Jingle Bells' was originally written for Thanksgiving?" Felice asked, her voice like a melody itself.

Mike took in her bright blue eyes and wavy blonde hair that seemed to shimmer under the streetlights. Snowflakes danced around them as he walked her home from choir practice. Their breaths turned into tiny clouds that mingled together in the evening air. The small town was adorned with twinkling lights and festive decorations, casting a warm glow on the salt and snow-covered streets below.

"Really? I didn't know that."

"Yep," she said with a grin. "It's funny how things change over time. Now it's one of the most popular Christmas songs."

Felice's cheeks flushed from the cold, making her even more radiant. Mike found himself drawn to everything about her, from the sound of her voice ringing clear in his ears to her attentiveness to the trivial things she knew about the holidays. It was rare to find someone who could make him feel so at ease, especially given his insecurities about his hearing impairment.

As they strolled beneath the twinkling Christmas lights that adorned the small town's main street, their breath formed tiny clouds in the chilly air. The scent of freshly baked gingerbread from a nearby bakery tantalized their senses. Mike wondered if it was the bakery his mother had been trying to tell him about. He'd love to visit it during open hours with Felice.

"Did you ever think about pursuing a career in music?" Felice asked.

"Never really crossed my mind," Mike admitted, his hands shoved deep into his jacket pockets.

"Your voice is truly amazing. You could have been a professional."

"Thanks," he said, feeling his cheeks warm with a mix of pride and embarrassment.

"Mike, can I ask you something?"

"Sure. What's up?"

"What's your Christmas wish?" she asked earnestly.

At first, Mike thought he had misheard her. "My Christmas wish?" he echoed, convinced she was joking. "Isn't that a bit childish?"

"Childish? No, not at all," Felice insisted, her tone serious. "Everyone has something they're hoping for during the holidays."

Mike hesitated, his attraction to Felice making him cautious not to insult her. Internally, he weighed the risks of sharing his true wish—one he guarded fiercely. In the end, he chickened out. "You go first."

Felice pressed her lips together before continuing. "My Christmas wish is to have someone to kiss under the mistletoe."

The confession hung in the air between them like an unspoken request. He looked up, hoping for a sprig of the plant. All he saw were the pine needles of the town's Christmas tree.

"Your turn, Mike," Felice prompted gently, her eyes full of anticipation.

"Uh, well... I guess you could say my wish is a bit more personal," Mike deflected, rubbing the back of his neck.

He couldn't bring himself to admit that his

Christmas wish was to not lose his hearing. To have moved just a few feet over from the blast that had rocked his eardrums. Just those few feet and he might not be in this predicament. The idea of revealing such an intimate part of himself made him feel exposed and vulnerable.

"Fair enough," Felice conceded, offering a warm smile. She didn't press any further, respecting his boundaries.

The cold winter air nipped at their cheeks as they continued walking side by side, the snow crunching beneath their boots. The small town they called home was decked out for the holiday season, every storefront adorned with wreaths and festive decorations. It felt like something out of a holiday cartoon.

"Isn't it amazing how music can bring people together? Especially during the holidays. There's just something magical about it."

"Yeah, it is pretty incredible," Mike agreed, his mind entirely focused on Felice's eyes sparkling from the reflection of the twinkling lights. *Incredible.*

"Speaking of magical, I think your voice will add something special to our performance this year."

Mike didn't reply. He knew he'd messed up at practice. He'd been so anxious about getting off key that he'd gotten off beat instead. His mind had raced with worries about how to perform his best when he couldn't always hear the beat and the other singers. One thing he knew for sure was that he could always hear Felice just fine.

"Here we are," Felice announced, stopping in front of a charming, two-story house adorned with colorful Christmas lights and a wreath hung on the door, welcoming them.

"Thanks for walking me home, Mike," she added, her smile lighting up the night. "It's been really nice."

"Anytime," he answered, meaning that single word. He'd walk with her into the cold waves if she asked.

Felice hesitated, glancing up before gesturing for him to do the same. Following her gaze, Mike's eyes widened as he discovered they were standing beneath a sprig of mistletoe hanging from the eaves of her porch. His heart pounded in his chest, the memory of her Christmas wish echoing in his mind.

"Would you look at that?" Felice said softly, her gaze lingering on the green leaves and white berries.

Mike bit his lower lip. He was torn between his desire to kiss her and his fear of getting too close and revealing his hearing loss. When the moment stretched out too long, Felice's smile wavered. Then it fell completely.

"Good night, Mike," she said, the disappointment evident in her voice.

"Good night, Felice," he murmured, watching her disappear inside.

With Felice's door closed behind her, Mike took a deep breath, trying to steady himself. The scent of her perfume lingered in the air, mingling with the crisp winter chill. He glanced up at the mistletoe one last time before turning away.

The streets were quiet, save for the distant laughter of children playing in the snow. Each step he took echoed in the stillness, reminding him of the rhythm of the choir—a rhythm he'd struggled to keep up with due to his hearing loss. Maybe there was potential for something more with Felice. First, he had to confront his own fears and find a way to be honest with her. Deep down, he still held on to his one true wish for the holidays—to have his hearing completely restored.

CHAPTER SIX

Felice had pushed too hard. That's why Mike hadn't kissed her under the mistletoe last night. But she was a woman who knew what she wanted. Backing off was not her style, not when she had no designs of being a backup singer. Felice was meant for the spotlight, and she wanted to share the stage with Mike.

"Hey Felice," shouted her cousin, Joy, running up to join her. "I'm hanging up flyers for the toy drive. Will you give me a hand?"

"Of course."

The annual Honor Valley Toy Drive was for the kids at the military base. It had been going on since Felice, Joy, and their other cousin Holly had been in middle school when their class had learned that there were some military families that were food insecure and the parents sometimes didn't have enough for gifts under the tree. The girls had thought it was wrong for the families who sacrificed the most to have the least, and so they'd decided to do something about it.

Felice had organized the youth choir. Joy had taken on the toy drive. And Holly, who was an excellent cook, had organized a food pantry. This year, she was also in charge of a holiday dinner for kids on the base.

"You're in high spirits today," Joy said as they plastered a flier at the bus stop on Main Street. "What's going on?"

"Nothing, just enjoying the holiday season."

"I know that look," Joy insisted, nudging Felice playfully. "Come on, spill it."

"All right, all right," Felice conceded, a blush rising to her cheeks. "It's Mike Harrington."

"I know that name. Wasn't he in Chorus? He was a few grades ahead of us, right?"

Felice wasn't sure. She would have remembered a boy with those good looks and that resonant voice. She knew him now, and she wanted to know more.

"There's just something about him... I can't quite put my finger on it. But it feels like we're meant to be together."

"Whoa there, slow down," Joy cautioned, laughing. "Didn't he enlist? He could've only just gotten back into town, meaning you've only known him for a short while. Maybe give it some time before you start planning your future together."

"Of course, you're right," Felice admitted. "But it's just so hard not to get swept up in the magic of the season. Especially with the way he looks at me. It's like he can see right through me."

"Felice, you're a hopeless romantic," Joy said fondly, linking her arm with Felice's as they continued walking.

"Maybe so, but it's Christmas, and anything can happen."

"True," Joy agreed. "Just remember, the most important thing is to enjoy the moment and let things unfold naturally. Don't force it."

"I won't." Because she wouldn't have to. It was all going to happen naturally—just as she planned.

An hour later, Felice reached the church where their next choir practice would be held. She stood in the choir's practice room, the soft glow of fairy lights casting a warm, inviting atmosphere. The warm spice scent of baked gingerbread filled the air, bringing with it a sense of merriment and anticipation. She glanced over at Mike, his strong jaw set in determination as he focused on the sheet music before him. Despite the tension in the room, her heart fluttered at the sight of him.

"All right, everyone." Felice clapped her hands to get the choir's attention. "Let's start with 'Joy to the World,' and remember to focus on those consonants to end strong."

As the choir began singing, Felice couldn't help but steal glances at Mike. His deep, resonant voice filled the room, stirring emotions within her that she had never experienced before. His singing rose above all of the others. But as the song progressed, she noticed the occasional offbeat rhythm coming from Mike's direction. It was subtle, but enough for her keen ear to pick up on. As they neared the end of the song, Mike was off the beat by a good measure.

"Stop, stop." Mrs. Jenkins' steel-grey eyes narrowed as she fixed her gaze on Mike. "I'm sorry, but I have to say something."

The room fell silent, all eyes turning toward the stern older woman. Felice felt a knot form in her stomach, fearing what was about to come.

"We need to address the issue with Mike's timing."

Mike's eyes dropped to the floor, and his shoulders slumped.

There was a scratch of irritation in Felice's chest about Mrs. Jenkin's public criticism of him. Whenever Felice corrected anyone, she did it one on one, not making a spectacle of them. And she did that now.

"All right, everyone, let's take a moment," Felice called, silencing the choir with a gentle wave of her hand. She walked over to Mike, placing a comforting hand on his shoulder. "Singing in a choir is different from singing alone. It takes practice to blend in, to feel the music as a part of a group rather than an individual."

Mike looked up at her, uncertainty still shadowing his eyes.

"I hear something special in your voice, Mike. I believe in you. Let's practice together, just the two of us, until you get the hang of it. How does that sound?"

A grateful smile spread across his face. His eyes brightened.

"David, why don't you lead the group in the rest

of the songs, while I go work one on one with Mike?"

David smirked from behind Mrs. Jenkins, making kissy faces. Luckily, only Felice could see her childish brother.

In the sanctuary of the private practice room, Felice and Mike stood facing each other, their eyes locked, their voices intertwined in perfect harmony. Here, away from the critical eyes and ears of the others, Mike's timing was impeccable. His strong baritone matched Felice's melodic soprano, resonating with a chemistry that went beyond mere musical compatibility.

They moved closer together as the song progressed, the music a force pulling them as one, their voices a reflection of something deeper. Felice felt her heartbeat quicken. The warmth of Mike's breath mingled with hers as the distance between them diminished.

Her mind started to wander, and an unfamiliar excitement took hold. Was this the right moment? She found herself drawn to his eyes, his lips, the intensity of his expression as he sang. The urge to lean in, to steal a kiss from him, became nearly over-whelming.

Just as she was about to surrender to the impulse,

her peripheral vision caught movement in the door-way. A few choir members had gathered, their curious eyes watching the intimate duet. Reality snapped back, and Felice's courage faltered. The song ended, and the room was filled with a lingering silence, the echo of their voices still vibrating in the air.

"That was wonderful, Mike," Felice said, her voice slightly shaky, trying to regain her composure. "Your timing is perfect with me. I mean—maybe... maybe the pressure of the group was just a little over-whelming before."

"My timing's always perfect when I'm with you."

She swallowed hard. His throat worked, doing the same. There might not be a mistletoe hanging overhead, but there were onlookers hanging in the door. If it wasn't for them, Felice would've pushed all propriety away and stolen the kiss she so desired from this man. But she knew there would be other chances, other moments. If there was truly some-thing blossoming between them, it would find its way.

"Let's get back to the others," she suggested, her voice still tinged with the unspoken longing.

Mike nodded, and they walked back to the main room, their voices silent but their hearts speaking a language only they could hear. The connection they'd forged went beyond the music, beyond the practice room, and Felice felt certain that, in time, it would lead them to a harmony that had more than their voices mingling.

CHAPTER SEVEN

*A*s the final chord resonated through the space, Mike allowed himself a moment to appreciate the beauty of the music they had been creating together. He glanced over at Felice, whose smile seemed to encompass everyone in the room. Mike wanted it focused solely on him, on them, and the music they made together. She radiated a passion for music that was impossible not to admire, and Mike couldn't help but feel drawn to her.

It struck him then how easily he could hear Felice whenever she spoke or sang. Her voice seemed to reach him even when other sounds faded into the background. In those moments, he felt as if they were connected on a deeper level, as if her presence somehow made everything else fall into place.

As he walked out of the church, the warmth of Felice's presence lingered with him, mixed with the sting of embarrassment from earlier in the evening. He could still hear the accusatory tone of the choir member who'd called him out. He still felt the flush of shame that had risen to his cheeks.

He knew Felice had noticed that his timing was off. He'd been watching her and saw her frown in his direction. He had been watching her lips move and realized that he was a few words behind her. It was the only way he knew he was off the beat because listening to everyone else didn't sound as clear as her voice.

He wished they could just sing a duet together. The connection they'd forged in that private practice room was undeniable. And yet, he'd hesitated to take her offer to walk her home, a nagging fear holding him back.

His progressive sensorineural hearing loss was a deeply personal battle, one that he'd yet to fully come to terms with. He'd considered telling Felice, opening up to her about the fear and uncertainty that gnawed at him. But the words had stuck in his throat, the vulnerability too raw, too fresh.

As he made his way home, the cold winter air biting at his skin, Mike made a silent vow to himself.

He would figure this out, find the strength to face his fears, and when the time was right, he would open up to Felice.

It was unsurprising to him that the sound of his cellphone ringing the next morning woke him up when his alarm clock had failed at the same duty for the last couple of days. Spying the number on the face of the phone, Mike accepted the call and wished he couldn't hear the prognosis of the doctor on the other end.

Mike sat on the edge of his bed, phone pressed to his ear, as he waited for the Telehealth call to connect. The line clicked, and Dr. Williams, a military doctor whose reputation for sternness was offset by his compassion, came on the line.

It was a video call. Dr. Williams had even turned on the speech to text captions. Mike kept his gaze on the man's face and not on the white letters that sprawled across the bottom of his cell phone.

"I've reviewed your audiograms and consulted with some specialists," Dr. Williams began, his voice tinged with gravity that immediately caught Mike's attention. "I have to say, the news isn't great."

Mike clenched his jaw, bracing himself. "What are we looking at, sir?"

The doctor was a captain in the United States

Army, and Mike made sure to give him his due deference, even though Dr. Williams was about to deliver him bad news.

"Your hearing has already deteriorated, and it's likely to continue to get worse over time," Dr. Williams said in his no-nonsense way.

Mike paused, letting the words sink in. "All right, so what are my options? Hearing aids?"

Dr. Williams sighed on the other end of the line. "Hearing aids could be a temporary solution, but given the rate of your hearing loss, I think it would be wise to consider something more permanent. Have you ever thought about cochlear implants?"

"Cochlear implants? That's... that's a big step, isn't it?"

"It is, but considering the progressive nature of your condition, they might offer the best chance for you to regain some level of normal hearing."

"What's the timeline of something like this? Military red tape and all."

"That's the unfortunate part," Dr. Williams said. "The military healthcare system can be slow to approve these kinds of procedures. It could be a long wait—possibly a year or more."

"A year is a long time to wait when you can't hear well."

"If you have private insurance, the process could be expedited significantly."

"Thank you, sir," Mike said, his voice tinged with both gratitude and resignation. "I've got a lot to think about."

"Of course, Mike. Take your time, but not too much time if you want to get in line for the procedure with the military. I'll be here to answer any questions you may have moving forward."

Mike hung up the phone and set it down on the side table. The weight of the news settled over him like a thick fog, obscuring the future. He was surprised to find that the main line of his thinking kept leading him back to Felice.

He was faced with a dilemma that felt like a clash of loyalties—loyalty to himself and his self-esteem and loyalty to Felice, whose name came to his mind unbidden yet so naturally. Just thinking about her invoked an aching warmth, a fleeting comfort that he yearned to make permanent.

They had only two weeks until the choir's Christmas performance—a performance meant to lift the spirits of the children and families on the military base, a performance that was much more than just singing notes on a page. There was no way he would get the operation in time, even if he hustled with private insurance.

He took out his phone, his thumb hovering over Felice's name. She had faith in him; her eyes sparkled like the North Star whenever they practiced. But could faith correct timing, tune, or the syncopation of voices harmonizing? Could it mask the hesitation he felt every time he had to sing in the choir, each note like walking a tightrope?

His thumb tapped aimlessly on the screen, indecisive. To tell Felice would be to admit his limitations. To quit the choir would mean letting everyone down, including her. And to continue without saying a word? That would be the grandest lie of them all—one that might reach its crescendo in a very public, heartbreaking spectacle.

CHAPTER EIGHT

nowflakes danced outside the window as Felice sat in her living room, a steaming cup of hot cocoa warming her hands. She glanced at the clock on the mantel, watching its long hand move, anticipating the arrival of her guest. She smoothed out her festive red dress and took a deep breath.

David lounged on the living room couch. His attention was glued to the television as he tinkered with his latest creation. The kid hadn't taken a hint that Felice wanted privacy. So it was time to be blunt.

"David," she called, her voice a touch more forceful than she intended, "I need the living room for a while. Can you take your video game to your room?"

"It's not a video game. I'm coding."

"Whatever. Take it to your room, please."

David looked up, an annoyed expression on his face. One glance at his sister's serious demeanor made him relent. "Fine, fine," he grumbled, gathering his devices.

A soft knock on the door pulled Felice from her thoughts, and she hurried to open it. There stood Mike Harrington, his athletic frame bundled in a thick winter coat, his short-cropped brown hair dusted with snow. His somber expression softened when he saw Felice's bright smile.

"Come on in and get warm." Felice stepped aside to let him enter.

"Thanks, Felice."

Mike's deep voice resonated despite the hesitancy she saw in his eyes. As he removed his coat, there was a slight tension in his shoulders. He had texted her last night that he wanted to talk with her in private. As she motioned for him to sit on the couch, her smile of expectation froze on her lips. Mike was standing there, his hands shoved into his pockets, his face etched with hesitancy and doubt.

This didn't look like the face of a man about to make romantic overtures.

"Is everything okay?" Felice asked, concern replacing her earlier anticipation.

"I just needed to talk to you about something." His voice was tight, his expression guarded.

Whatever was on Mike's mind, it was clear that this wasn't going to be the conversation she'd hoped for. The chemistry she'd felt, the connection that had seemed so real, now hung in the balance, overshadowed by the doubt in Mike's eyes. But she was ready to listen, ready to understand, no matter what the situation might be.

Mike fidgeted with the hem of his shirt, his eyes downcast, his face etched with a vulnerability she had seen before when Mrs. Jenkins had called him out in front of the entire choir for being out of synch.

"Mike?" she prompted gently, her voice soft and encouraging.

His head jerked up to her immediately. His gaze searched hers as though he'd lost something in her eyes. "I'm sorry. What did you say?"

"Nothing. I just called your name."

Mike took in a deep breath and let it out. His gaze never left her lips. He was giving all kinds of mixed signals. Did he want to kiss her? Or tell her the world was about to end?

"Whatever it is, you can tell me."

"Felice, the reason I've been having trouble with timing in the choir... it's not because I'm new to singing in a group. It's because I'm losing my hearing."

The words hung in the air, a shock that reverberated through the room. Felice's mind struggled to process what he'd just said, her earlier fantasies of romance crumbling in the face of this unexpected revelation.

"You're... losing your hearing?" she repeated, her voice barely above a whisper, the weight of his words sinking in.

Mike sat down, his face pale, his eyes filled with a sadness that pierced her heart. "It's progressive sensorineural hearing loss. It started after an explosion while I was in the military, and it's been getting worse."

Without thinking, she reached for his right ear. Then she pulled her hand back before she could cup his face. A formed lump in her throat, a mixture of sympathy, shock, and a profound sense of empathy for what he must be going through. All thoughts of romance were forgotten, replaced by a desire to be there for her friend, to support him in this painful and personal struggle.

"I'm so sorry," she said, reaching out to take his hand. "I can't imagine how hard this must be for you."

He squeezed her hand, his eyes leaving her mouth and finally meeting hers. It hadn't been mixed signals. He'd been trying to ensure he heard her when she spoke.

"I wanted you to know. I didn't want to keep it a secret from you, especially after... after how you stuck up for me in choir practice."

"Is there nothing that can be done?"

"I'm going to need cochlear implants. It won't happen for some time. That's why I've decided to step down from the choir."

"No," she said immediately. Possibly too loudly.

"You don't have to shout." He grinned. "At least not yet. I can hear you fine. In fact, you're the only person I seem to have no trouble hearing."

The last part was said more to himself than anything. Felice was far too focused on the part where he was quitting the choir.

"I don't want you to give up choir. Your voice is too beautiful."

"You've heard me in the group. I don't want to throw off the performance."

"Maybe a solo?"

He shook his head.

"How about a duet… just you and me?"

He didn't deny that idea so quickly.

"I can tap your hand to help you keep the beat while we sing. That way, we'll stay in sync throughout the entire song."

She still had hold of his hand. She tapped out a little melody against the fleshy part of his thumb to demonstrate. But she quickly lost the timing as the warmth of their hands touching sent a jolt through her heart. And then she began to sing.

Her voice rang out a clear and melodic tune. She started up the tapping again, beating out the rhythm against the back of Mike's hand. Each tap was deliberate and confident, and she urged him to join in.

Mike hesitated for a moment. He watched her lips move. Then he looked down at her fingers, as though trying to concentrate on the sensation of Felice's touch. He drew in a steadying breath before joining in. When he did, his deep, resonant voice blended perfectly with Felice's soprano.

They sang together, their voices dancing around one another like snowflakes caught in a winter breeze. Felice continued to tap out the rhythm on Mike's hand, her focus never wavering. She felt his grip tighten slightly as they hit the chorus, a silent acknowledgement that he appreciated her guidance.

As their voices rose and fell in perfect harmony, Felice found herself drawn to Mike's face, watching the way his eyes lit up as they sang, the way his lips formed each note with precision and passion.

Her gaze fell to his lips. Her heart beat faster. A longing built inside her.

"Wow," Mike whispered as the last note of their duet faded away. "I didn't think it was possible for us to sound so... perfect together."

"Anything is possible if you have faith and someone by your side. You don't have to face this alone, Mike. I'm here for you."

The silence that followed was like the pause between movements in a symphony, a moment of anticipation, a space filled with potential. They sat close, their breaths coming in measured beats, the rhythm of their hearts pulsing in a shared tempo.

There was no mistletoe in sight, no excuse for a stolen kiss. Yet the desire was there. A longing had built inside of Felice that was as poignant as a minor key. She dared to look into Mike's eyes, searching for some sign that he felt the same way.

Then, as if responding to an unspoken melody, Mike leaned in. His movement was smooth and graceful, like the slide of a bow across violin strings. Their lips came together in a kiss that was a crescendo building.

It was a kiss that sang. It was a refrain they'd been building to. The sigh that escaped Felice's mouth as Mike deepened the kiss was a note in a song that had been waiting to be sung. Their relationship was a composition they were writing together, a melody that was uniquely theirs.

As they pulled apart, their eyes met, smiles breaking across their faces like the final triumphant chords of a beloved piece. They didn't need words; their feelings were composed in the music they'd created together, a symphony of connection that had only just begun.

CHAPTER NINE

Mike pulled up to Felice's house, his hands gripping the steering wheel a little tighter than necessary. The anticipation of their evening together had been building all day. His palms were sweaty as he shifted into park. He took a deep breath, reminding himself that he'd planned everything meticulously—from the location to the decorations.

As he approached the door, he heard laughter and music coming from inside the Evergreen household. He hesitated for a moment before raising his hand to knock. Before his knuckles even brushed the door, it swung open to reveal David grinning widely.

"Hey, Mike. You're right on time," David said,

adjusting his glasses with one hand while clutching a tablet in the other. "Felice will be ready in a sec."

David was enunciating his words and projecting his voice just a touch louder than he had the day before. Clearly Felice had told her brother about his hearing loss. The thought didn't bother Mike.

"How are things going with your latest tech project?" Mike indicated the tablet in the young man's hand.

"Awesome. I just finished coding a new app. I'll show you sometime."

"Sounds great, man," Mike said, genuinely interested.

A soft click echoed through the hallway. All interest in games and tablets fled as Mike's attention was immediately drawn to Felice. She appeared in the doorway wearing a stunning green dress. Her blue eyes twinkled when she saw him, and her smile lit up the room.

He wanted to kiss her again. He'd been thinking of nothing but the feel of her lips against his, the taste of her, and the sound she made when he'd pulled her close. But that would be highly improper to do in front of her little brother.

"Ready to go?" she asked.

"Absolutely," he replied, offering her his arm.

"Have fun, you two," David called after them as they made their way to Mike's car.

Once settled in the car, Mike glanced over at Felice and smiled. "I have something special planned for tonight. I hope you'll like it."

"I can't wait to see what it is."

Twenty minutes later, Mike pulled up to their destination. The sun had just set, casting a soft glow across the sky. He helped her out of the car, her hand feeling warm in his.

"Wow, Mike," Felice breathed as she took in the scene before them. "This is so beautiful."

He'd had spent hours setting up the perfect romantic date. A cozy picnic blanket lay on the sand, surrounded by flickering candles nestled in the small dunes he'd constructed. Fairy lights were strung up around the area, casting a warm, inviting light.

"Remember this place?" he asked, leading her toward the setup.

"Of course. This is where we first met," she replied with a wide smile.

"I thought it would be special to come back here for our first date."

Felice's eyes sparkled as the two of them sat down on the blanket. In the center, a small bouquet of flowers rested alongside a scattering of rose petals. The fragrant scent mingled with the saltiness of the crashing waves.

"Mike, you really went above and beyond."

"Of course I did. It's for you."

The roaring fire nearby crackled and danced, providing warmth against the chill of the winter night. They sat close, letting the heat from the flames envelop them. The scent of the water mingled with the aroma of burning wood and rose petals, creating a heady atmosphere that enveloped them both. Felice leaned closer to Mike, her breath warm against his ear as she told him about her dreams and aspirations.

"Ever since I was a little girl, I wanted to share my love for music with others," she told him. "I want our choir to bring joy and happiness to people during the holiday season, and maybe even inspire others to find their own passions."

Mike listened intently, nodding along as he felt a surge of admiration for her dedication and enthusiasm. He smiled at the thought of Felice leading her choir to success. The image of her standing proudly in front of her singers filled him with a warmth that spread through his chest like hot chocolate on a winter's day.

"I have no doubt you'll achieve everything you set your mind to."

"What about you?" she asked. "What are your dreams?"

He hesitated for a moment, feeling a pang of vulnerability at the question. "I... I want to find a new purpose in life. After leaving the military, I've struggled to figure out what comes next. I want to help others, but sometimes it feels like an impossible task."

"Your strength and resilience are remarkable, Mike. Whatever path you choose, I know you'll make a meaningful impact."

Mike watched the firelight dance across Felice's face, casting a warm glow on her delicate features. He was drawn to her bright blue eyes, which sparkled like the stars above them. As they sat together on the picnic blanket, their conversation flowed effortlessly, and Mike sensed that their connection was deepening with each shared story and dream.

She told him about her large family who were obsessed with Christmas. Each branch of the Ever-greens had a habit of naming their children something holiday themed; hence Felice and Navidad. But she made Mike swear never to call her brother by his legal name.

Mike told her about his work as an Army medic. The young private who'd stepped on an IED but survived, thanks to Mike's quick response. About a fellow medic he'd helped save by improvising a tourniquet out of a torn uniform. He didn't share the stories of the countless locals whose lives were forever changed by conflict and the children he couldn't always help due to lack of materials and supplies. Instead, he spoke about the sense of brotherhood and duty that kept him going even when things seemed unbearable.

Felice reached out and gently took Mike's hand in hers, intertwining their fingers. The simple touch sent a shiver down his spine. He marveled at the warmth and strength he found in her grasp. For the first time in a long time, Mike began to believe in the power of Christmas again because Santa had just delivered the thing on his Christmas list Mike hadn't even thought to ask for.

CHAPTER TEN

The choir's voices rang out in harmony. The dimly lit room sparkled with the infusion of their Christmas carol. Felice only had eyes and ears for one choral member.

She caught Mike's gaze as they sang together in their duet. Her soprano soared above the ensemble, while his baritone brought depth to their sound. They held hands for effect, but in truth, Felice tapped out the rhythm for him, helping him to keep time. Mike didn't miss a beat.

"Sing, choirs of angels," she continued, her gaze locked with Mike's as they navigated the song together. It was as if the rest of the world had fallen away, leaving only the two of them wrapped up in the magic of the moment.

"O come, let us adore Him, Christ the Lord," they finished together, the final note echoing through the hushed room. As the choir members erupted into applause, Mrs. Jenkins included, Felice felt a smug surge of pride for Mike's performance.

"Wow," whispered Mrs. Jenkins, tears glistening in her eyes. "That was simply beautiful."

"Amazing job, you two," Mary chimed in, clapping enthusiastically.

"See?" Felice said softly, squeezing Mike's hand. "You belong here, just as much as any of us."

"I couldn't have done it without you," he replied, his voice thick with emotion.

"Thank you, everyone," Felice said as the applause quieted. "Let's keep up this momentum and make our Christmas performance one to remember."

With renewed energy, the choir resumed practice, buoyed by the memory of the duet that had captured their hearts and filled them with hope. Mike took a place at the front of the choir, where he could see and hear her. This was their plan for when they weren't singing a duet.

The choir room was alive with activity as they launched into their final run-through of the evening. Every voice was in perfect harmony and perfect time. Felice glanced over at Mike, who wore an expression of determination and focus mixed with a hint of vulnerability. She offered him a reassuring smile.

Okay, it was more of an *I told you so* smile. Because she had told him so. She'd told him he could do this. That they could do this. And she'd been right.

Then, just as they were about to hit the last chord of "Mele Kalikimaka," a challenging Hawaiian Christmas song made popular by Bing Crosby, Mike's voice wavered. The song was fast-paced, and he missed the note. His voice rang out loud in the silence of the other choir members, taking a breath. The sound hung in the air, a jarring discordance amidst the harmony.

Mike's face drained of color, his eyes wide and panicked. The room was filled with a tense silence, the weight of the error hanging heavily in the air.

Felice wanted to rush to him, to comfort him, to tell him it was all right. Before she could move, Mike's shoulders slumped, and he began to move. He wasn't moving toward her. He backed up through the chorus members, heading for the door.

There were too many people between him and

Felice. She stood at the front of the room, torn between her responsibility to the choir and her growing love for Mike. She knew that she had to find a way to make this right, to heal the wound that had been opened by that one missed beat.

"Felice, we all know how much this show means to the kids and families on the base," Mary said, her voice tinged with sorrow. "With the budget cuts and everything they've been going through, they need this. We need to uplift them, and we can't do that if we're not at our best. I worry that your feelings are crowding your judgment."

That was true. Her feelings were influencing her decisions, but the members didn't have all the information. They didn't know that Mike's hearing was going. They didn't realize how remarkable he was doing inspite of his hearing loss.

"Mike's a nice guy with a powerful voice, but maybe he could take a smaller role," said Mrs. Jenkins. "Something that won't affect the overall performance."

"This show is incredibly important," Felice said. "We all want it to be the best it can be. But we also have to remember that we're a team, a community, and sometimes that means supporting each other even when it's difficult."

The choir members exchanged glances. Their expressions were still filled with worry. In the end, each and every member nodded, trusting in Felice's judgment.

As they filed out of the room, Felice's eyes went to the opposite door Mike had backed himself through. She would stand by him, support him, help him find his way. With a deep breath, she headed for the door, determined to find Mike, to talk to him, to reassure him that they could still make this work.

But as she reached for the doorknob, a pang of fear struck her. What if he didn't want to hear what she had to say? What if he'd given up? What if the harmony they'd found was shattered by this one discordant moment?

Pushing the fear aside, she opened the door and stepped into the hallway. She would find a way to make this right; she had to. The music they'd created together was too beautiful to be silenced by one missed note.

Felice watched Mike as he stood in front of the church, his eyes distant, his body language betraying his disconnection from the joyous scene around him. The laughter of children and the festive jingling of sleigh bells filled the crisp winter air, but Mike

seemed unable to fully immerse himself in the celebration.

Her heart ached for him, knowing that his
hearing loss was creating an invisible barrier
between him and the world. The beautiful complexi-
ties of sound were becoming muddled and distorted
for him, turning joy into confusion.

"Mike?" she called, her voice cutting through the
noise. She waved to him from the top of the church
steps, her voice soft but warm, hoping to reach him.
"Mike, are you all right?"

He didn't respond at first. She didn't want to yell,
so she got closer before she called again, making
sure she was in his line of sight.

"Hey," he said, forcing a smile as he turned to her.

"Did you hear what I said?" she asked, knowing
him well enough to see through his facade.

"I'm sorry for running out like that," he stammered, his voice tinged with embarrassment. "I just
couldn't keep up with that song."

Felice grasped his hands in hers. "Mike, it's okay.
We'll practice more, we'll get through this together.
You have such a beautiful voice; you were born to
sing."

"Sure," he replied, his voice hollow.

The word was a lie, and they both knew it. He

was no longer the confident baritone with a rich and resonant voice. That man had become a shadow, and in his place stood someone quiet, unsure.

"My hearing... it's not just affecting my singing. It's changing everything. I don't feel like myself anymore. How can I sing when I can't even hear the music like I used to? How can I be a part of the choir when I feel so lost?"

Felice pulled back, cupping his face in her hands, forcing him to look at her. "You're not lost, Mike. You're here with me, and we'll face this together. Your voice is still beautiful, even if things are different now. And I still believe in you, more than anything."

"Felice," he whispered, his voice cracking with emotion, "I don't think I can do this anymore."

Her eyes had filled with unshed tears as she pleaded with him not to give up. But she knew, deep down, that he had reached a painful realization. He needed to find a new way to connect, a way that didn't rely on the sounds that were slipping away from him.

She forced a smile in return, masking her own pain and uncertainty. How could she help him find his place again? How could she support him without becoming a crutch?

As they stood together, surrounded by the sounds of celebration, Felice knew that they would have to navigate this new and uncertain path together. The music that had once united them had changed, but she was determined to find a new harmony, one that would resonate with both of them, no matter what lay ahead.

CHAPTER ELEVEN

"From what I can see here, your hearing loss is quite severe, around 70 decibels. At this level, I'm afraid there aren't many non-surgical options left to consider."

Mike wanted to pretend he hadn't heard the private audiologist, but the man was seated right next to his ear. The warm lighting cast a soft glow over the bookshelves filled with medical texts and various ear-related decorations. Even if he hadn't heard, his mom sat in one of the waiting chairs, her hands fidgeting nervously in her lap. Felice stood beside him, holding his hand with steady fingers.

Even though he'd decided to leave the choir, he had hoped to hold on to her. He had to admit that he'd been surprised the thought of her leaving him hadn't crossed her mind. After the disastrous practice, she'd taken him out for a consoling cup of hot chocolate at one of the local coffee shops, Sandy Perk. Hot chocolate, Felice assured him, was the cure for everything. Too bad it couldn't fix his eardrums.

It was the was news. His hearing loss had not only robbed him of his career, but also threatened to take away his passion for music. Mike knew that there was no easy solution. Still, he couldn't help hoping for a miracle.

"Are you saying there's nothing we can do?" said Felice.

Dr. Foster shook his head, his expression somber. "I wish there were more I could offer you. But given the severity of hearing loss, a cochlear implant operation is likely the only viable solution to prevent further damage. There's a clinic in New York City that specializes in the procedure. They're one of the best in the country, and I think they could give you the help you need."

"New York City?" Mike asked, feeling a glimmer of hope. "Is it by chance a VA clinic?"

The doctor winced. "It's private care. Which I'm sure I don't have to tell you can be very expensive, and there's usually a waiting list. The operation itself can cost upwards of $50,000."

Mike couldn't afford that, not without going into crippling debt. He stared at the floor. His mind raced with questions and doubts about his future.

Dr. Foster placed a comforting hand on his shoulder. "I know this is a lot to take in, but you don't have to make any decisions right now. Take some time to think things over and talk to your loved ones. Looks like you've got an army on your side. I'm confident you'll find a way through this."

Mike stumbled out of the doctor's office, the world spinning around him. His mother and Felice followed close behind, their faces etched with concern. The winter air was crisp, filled with the distant laughter of children and the faint hum of traffic. The smells of a nearby bakery wafted through the air, mingling with the sharp scent of car exhaust.

He felt his mother's hand on his shoulder. He knew it was hers because she gave him a shake, like he was being a naughty child. She must have called his name more than once by the worry she failed to hide.

"Mike, sweetheart, we'll figure this out."

Felice took his hand, her touch warm and reassuring. "And I'll be right … every step of the way. You're … Mike. You can …."

Felice's voice had always been the strongest in his ears. Now it was muted and distant, as if he were tuning a radio, the volume dial of her voice turning up and down. Mike's palms were sweaty. He felt a crushing weight on his chest, as though the very air were being sucked out of him.

"I don't want to be strong," he snapped, the words tasting bitter in his mouth. He shook his head, the world tilting. "You don't understand. It's like I'm losing myself, piece by piece."

"Your singing voice… still a … you. They're still…"

He stared hard at Felice's lips. Lips he'd kissed just this morning as she came to his house to accompany them on this ill-fated appointment. He wanted to take comfort in her words. But he couldn't even hear them all. The fear was a cold, hard knot in his stomach, twisting and tightening. He pulled away, the world blurring, their voices fading in and out like a bad radio signal.

He knew they meant well. He knew they loved him. Well, he knew his mom loved him. Felice cared. But would she care when he could no longer hear her at all? When he could no longer hear the music that was as much a part of her as her soul?

He didn't think she would. He didn't think she

should. He didn't want to give up the music. He couldn't ask her to do it for him. Not when he was coming to love her as much as he loved his favorite melody.

He should break it off with her. Right now, before it got too painful. But he couldn't form the words. Right now, all he wanted was to escape, to find a quiet place where he could come to terms with the new reality that was closing in around him.

"I need to think. I need to breathe. Please, just give me some space."

And with that, he turned and walked away, leaving behind the two women who loved him most. The world closed in around him, the sounds and smells of the city dull and distant. All he could hear was the roar of his own fear, the endless silence that threatened to consume him.

CHAPTER TWELVE

Felice settled into the plush booth at her favorite coffee shop. She'd been coming to Sandy Perk since she could hold a mug of hot chocolate in her hands. Right now, her hands trembled as she cradled a steaming mug of spiced chai latte. The rich aroma of roasted coffee beans and freshly baked pastries filled the air, mingling with the soft murmur of conversation and the occasional clinking of cups and saucers.

Across from her, Joy and Holly watched her closely, their faces filled with concern. Her cousins knew something was wrong.

"Spill it, Fe," Holly said, leaning forward. Her eyes, sharp and observant, missed nothing.

"Yeah, you've been holding back all day," Joy

175

added, her voice gentle. She reached across the table and placed a comforting hand over Felice's. "Whatever it is, we're here for you."

Felice took a deep breath, her heart aching as she thought of Mike. How could she put into words the turmoil of emotions she was feeling? The love, the fear, the uncertainty?

"Mike's losing his hearing," she said finally, the words catching in her throat. "He's been struggling for a while now, but it's getting worse. He's scared, and I'm pretty sure he's going to try and play martyr and break up with me."

Joy and Holly exchanged a glance, their faces filled with shock and sympathy.

"Oh, Felice, that's awful," Holly said, her voice cracking. "But you believe in him. You can help him through this."

"I know I can," Felice said. "But he's pulling away. He's so proud, and he's always been so independent. Now he feels like he's losing control of his life, and he doesn't know how to handle it."

"Maybe he just needs some time," Joy suggested. "He's probably feeling vulnerable and overwhelmed right now. Give him some space but let him know you're there for him. Show him that his hearing loss doesn't change how you feel about him."

"And don't forget to take care of yourself," Holly added. "This is going to be a difficult journey for both of you. Make sure you have the support you need, too."

Of course an Evergreen girl would say that. The Christmas-obsessed family who believed in helping others didn't skimp on self-care. These two knew her, they understood her, and they always had the right words to say.

"Thank you," Felice said, squeezing the hands of both women. "I don't know what I'd do without you two."

Mike was the one. Felice knew it in her heart. Santa had brought her the perfect gift a full two weeks early. And no matter what obstacles they faced, she would stand by him, loving him and supporting him every step of the way.

"How's the toy drive going?" she asked Joy.

"You will not believe who's back in town," Joy said, her hackles going up. But her hackles were raised at the same time as her nostrils seemed to flare with desire. "Lucas Jackson."

Lucas was the love of Joy's life. Granted, Joy was only twenty-four, like both Felice and Holly. But since they were kids, Joy Evergreen and Lucas Jackson had been inseparable. That is until he went off to join the military and left her behind.

"I guess it's a time for a lot of hometown boys to return this season," said Holly. "Ryan Blake's back too."

Ryan was Holly's older brother's best friend. Ever since Holly started dating when she was sixteen, she'd held every would-be suitor up to Ryan's standard. But what teenager could have ever measured up to a twenty-six-year-old grown man?

The pleasant hum of conversation and the soothing background music were suddenly interrupted by a loud, jarring noise. Felice, Joy, and Holly all jumped, looking around for the source of the sound.

"What on earth was that?" Joy's hand was on her chest as if to calm her racing heart.

Felice's gaze darted to the corner of the café, where her brother David was tinkering with a complex-looking device.

"Sorry, guys," he said. "My bad."

"What is that?" asked Holly.

"It's my new invention I'm working on in tech class. It uses Bluetooth to amplify specific sounds, like music or voices."

"Can you turn it off?" said Joy. "It's making a lot of noise."

"It's not supposed to," said David. "It's just supposed to pulse and give off a signal."

Pulse and give off a signal? Using Bluetooth? Joy leaped up from the booth and hurried over to David, her mind racing with the possibilities.

"David, do you think you could fine-tune that device to keep time to music?"

David looked up, his face lighting up with interest. She didn't have to say who the alterations were for. Her brother understood her perfectly. "You think it could help him?"

Joy and Holly joined them, their faces filled with curiosity as they crowded around David's device.

"Anything that could help Mike would be worth trying," Felice said. "Even if it's just a temporary solution, it could make a world of difference to him."

David's eyes sparkled with enthusiasm as he began to explain the mechanics of his invention, the excitement in his voice contagious. "I think I can modify it to focus on certain frequencies, like the ones that Mike's struggling with. It might take some time and a lot of testing, but I think it's possible."

This could be the breakthrough they needed, the key to helping Mike regain his confidence and reconnect with the world around him. She turned to Joy and Holly, her eyes shining with gratitude and excitement. Her friends' faces lit up with smiles, their eyes filled with understanding and support.

"Then let's do it," Felice said. "Let's help Mike get back to doing what he loves."

CHAPTER THIRTEEN

Mike slammed the door to the rental car. He nodded and waved after handing the keys back to the salesman, pretending he was in a rush and couldn't spare a moment to hear the man's sales pitch on purchasing the car. In truth, Mike could barely hear a word the man had said.

Spending three days out camping had seemed like a good idea after hearing about his prognosis. But the silence in the cold woods had proved a living nightmare. Mike came to realize he hated being alone even more than the quiet.

Now he stood in the center of the festively decorated town square, feeling a heavy weight on his chest. All around him, the cheerful townsfolk chatted excitedly with one another while doing a last grab at holiday shopping. The only chatter Mike wanted to hear was the sweet notes of Felice's voice. He'd even let his mother pester him and his dad go on about the antiques shows he loved.

The air was crisp and cold, carrying the scent of cinnamon and pine that reminded him of happier times. But those memories were bittersweet now, tainted by the absence of Felice's warm laughter and her gentle touch on his arm as they practiced their harmonies together.

He'd been out in a dead zone when he'd gone camping, so there had been no cellphone contact. The moment he got near a cell tower, his phone beeped to life, alerting him to the dozens of messages she'd left him.

I have something to tell you.

Can we talk?

Are you okay?

I miss you.

And then nothing. The silence of the text messages was far too loud. Had he blown it?

The snowflakes gently fell around him. Red, green, and yellow holiday lights twinkled at him from shop windows. Mistletoe dangled from every lamppost as he walked aimlessly down the street.

Mike realized his movements weren't aimless. He had a direction. His walk ended at Felice's doorstep.

He rang the doorbell and waited. No one answered.

A ringing started in his ear. He didn't want to believe it was too late. He didn't want to face that there was nothing he could do to win back the woman he'd fallen hard for. The ringing persisted. Then he realized it was coming from his pocket.

"Mike, I'm glad I caught you." Captain Williams wore a smile on his typically stern face over the video call. "I've got some great news for you, buddy."

Curiosity momentarily overshadowed Mike's melancholy. "What's that, sir?"

"It took some doing, but we managed to get your appeal for cochlear implants approved."

The words Dr. Williams spoke flashed across the screen seconds after his lips moved. Otherwise, Mike would have been sure he hadn't heard the man right.

"Approved?"

"Once the board was informed about your valor in the last mission, we were able to get you fast tracked."

"I'm approved?" Mike repeated, still not believing his eyes or his ears.

SHANAE JOHNSON

As Mike absorbed the implications of the news, his spirits began to lift. The world around him took on a new hue. He looked up at the mistletoe that hung on Felice's porch. He'd failed to kiss the woman he loved that first night. Now that he had a second chance to be able to hear, he would heed the call of love. He would never doubt the magic of the holidays again, having this miracle gifted to him.

"You deserve this, Mike. And it's a quick turn-around. They can slot you in early in the spring."

Spring? Months away. Long after the Christmas Carol concert.

Still, Mike cleared his throat and said, "Thank you, sir."

As Mike hung up the phone, his fingers trembled slightly against the screen door. A whirlwind of emotions swept through him. For a moment, he had been on top of the world. The approval of the operation had been a beacon of hope that promised to rewrite the future he'd almost resigned himself to. His future was brighter, but he'd have to wait a few more months in the darkness of silence.

"Mike!"

Mike looked up at the sound of his name. The person standing in front of him had the same blond hair, the same blue eyes, the same open smile as

184

Felice. David took the steps two by two until he was standing toe to toe with Mike.

"Where have you been? I've been looking for you, man. I made something for you."

David didn't give Mike a chance to answer any of his rapid-fire questions. He held out a small contraption in his hands. It resembled a makeshift hearing aid, fashioned from spare electronic components and a tiny speaker wrapped in a band.

"Put it on," David urged, his eyes sparkling with anticipation. "It's not as good as the implants will be when you get the operation, but it should help you hear better."

"How did you know I got approved for the cochlear implant operation?"

"You did? That's awesome, man. I didn't know. Fe asked me to make this for you. But then your mom said you were out camping when I stopped by to give it to you."

Mike winced at the last statement David made. Not because of his absence. Because David had been speaking at a higher than natural volume in an effort to compensate for Mike's hearing loss. But with the device in his ear, Mike heard him loud and clear. Emphasis on the loud part.

The device wasn't perfect. There was static that

made a buzzing sound. And the modulation wasn't steady. But it was better than his current reality.

"You made these?"

David nodded.

"You're a genius."

Again, the kid nodded. "Now you'll be able to sing at the Christmas carol event. Fe will be over the moon."

Just the sound of her name had Mike's heart racing. But when David pulled out his cell phone to text his sister, Mike stayed the young man's hand.

"She doesn't know I'm back. Let's keep it that way until the concert."

A grin spread across David's face. He put away his cellphone, and the two began to plan.

CHAPTER FOURTEEN

Felice paced back and forth in the dimly lit room behind the church's stage. Her favorite scent, the prickly pine of a Christmas tree, filled the air, but it did little to calm her nerves. She glanced at her choir members, who were huddled together in various stages of readiness. Some were looking at the exit sign, others continually clearing raspy throats.

"Okay, everyone," she said, trying to keep her voice steady. "We can do this. We've practiced for weeks, and we all know our parts."

But her eyes couldn't help but dart to the empty space where Mike should have been standing. His strong baritone voice had been the foundation that the choir needed. His absence felt like a gaping hole in their harmony.

"Felice, we all know how important this performance is to you," said Mrs. Jenkins, her hands wringing. "Without Mike, it just won't be the same. And we're sorry if we chased him away."

"You didn't chase him away." Felice took in a deep breath. "Mike suffered an injury during his last deployment that affected his ears. He's losing his hearing."

Gasps went around the room. There were glances of sorrow, looks of shame.

"After this performance, we're going to find him and get him back," insisted Mrs. Jenkins. "All of us."

Felice couldn't agree more. She would be the one leading that charge. But first, they had to get through this concert.

Gathering her courage, Felice led her choir members down the aisle of the church, their footsteps echoing softly on the wooden floor. The flickering candlelight cast a warm glow over the pews filled with expectant faces. Despite Mike's absence, she felt a surge of determination wash over her.

She glanced at the choir members, their expressions a mix of nerves and resolve. With a nod, Felice turned to face the audience, taking in the sight of familiar faces—neighbors, friends, and family—all waiting to be enchanted by the harmonies of their small-town choir.

As the piano introduction began, Felice looked out over the crowd, her gaze searching for one person in particular. She knew it was unlikely he would be there, but she couldn't help but hope. And then, as if a Christmas miracle unfolded before her eyes, she spotted him.

There, in the back row, sat Mike Harrington. His jaw was set. His brown eyes met hers with an intensity that sent a shiver down her spine. He offered her a tentative smile, the corners of his mouth lifting ever so slightly, and Felice knew in that moment that everything was going to be all right. As if responding to her thoughts, Mike gave her a subtle nod of encouragement to begin.

Taking a deep breath, she began to sing, her voice soaring through the church's rafters. The other choir members joined in, their harmonies melding together in a tapestry of sound that captivated the audience.

As they sang, Felice stole glances at Mike. Though he wasn't singing alongside her, the mere sight of him in the audience gave her the strength to pour every ounce of emotion into her performance.

"Silent night, holy night, all is calm, all is bright..."

Felice's voice rang out clear and strong. She poured her soul into each note. The audience watched, their rapt attention signaling that they, too, felt the power of the moment.

She looked again at Mike... but he was gone. She couldn't see him. But then she heard him.

"Round yon virgin, mother and child, holy infant, so tender and mild..."

She turned to the side of the room, and there he stood, walking toward her. The room seemed to hold its collective breath as he launched into the second verse, joining Felice in their duet.

"Sleep in heavenly peace, sleep in heavenly peace..."

His deep, resonant voice filled the church, effortlessly matching Felice's soprano. Though they were physically apart, their voices intertwined and danced through the air, creating a mesmerizing harmony.

Smiles spread across the faces of the choir members and audience alike as the magic of the moment washed over them. Felice felt tears prick at the corners of her eyes, but she refused to let them fall, determined to maintain the connection with Mike.

As they continued singing, Felice marveled at the synchronicity between them. Even without her there to tap the beat for him, Mike was keeping perfect time. His voice rang true, unwavering and strong. It was as if their shared passion for music had created an unbreakable bond that transcended his hearing loss.

"Christ, the Savior is born, Christ, the Savior is born..."

Together, they sang the final lines of the song. As the last note hung in the air, he reached her. He took his hand in hers, lacing their fingers together as though it was a representation of the bond they shared.

The audience leapt to their feet in a standing ovation. As Felice and Mike stood before each other, something unspoken passed between them, transcending words and filling the space with the electricity of connection. That's when she noticed the small, discreet Bluetooth device nestled in his ear.

"Bravo," shouted an elderly woman from the front row, her hands clapping vigorously. "Absolutely beautiful."

"Did you hear that, Mike?" Felice whispered, grinning ear to ear. "They loved it."

"Did you hear that I love you, Felice?" He raised

Felice's hand to his lips and pressed a gentle kiss to her knuckles.

There was no mistletoe. There was no bow to pull off a package. Still, Felice realized she was getting her Christmas wish at this moment. As the applause continued, Felice knew that this Christmas would be one she'd never forget—a night filled with love, laughter, and the sweetest music she'd ever heard.

"I need to apologize," he said.

"Apologize?" she asked, her eyebrows knitting together in confusion. "What for?"

"For how I acted when I first came back. I withdrew from you and the choir because of my insecurities. I let them control me, and I pushed away something that could have helped me heal. I love you, Felice. And I promise I won't let my insecurities come between us again."

As Felice gazed into Mike's warm brown eyes, she knew that together, they had created something truly special. Once withdrawn and somber, the man she loved now found himself basking in the warmth of a community that had embraced him despite his insecurities. More than that, he had risen above his fears and doubts to grant Felice her wish.

"Thank you, Santa."

"The name's Mike."

"Thank you, Santa, for bringing me Mike." Felice looked up toward the rafters as though she could see the jolly old man riding his sleigh in the night's sky. Instead, she saw something else.

Mike followed her gaze upward, where a sprig of mistletoe dangled precariously from the rafters above them. A mischievous grin spread across Felice's face, her eyes twinkling like stars against the night sky.

"Would you look at that?" she said.

"How on earth did it get up there?" Mike mused.

"Must be magic. Or maybe it's just good luck."

"Good luck, huh?" Mike looked into Felice's eyes. His gaze reflected the love and understanding that shone within them.

Slowly, tenderly, Mike leaned in and pressed his lips to hers. Their kiss captured the essence of their love in one sweet, lingering breath. Felice wanted to deepen the kiss, but this was a family show, and so she reluctantly pulled away and took a bow. With the community applauding them, she felt lost in a moment of pure joy. Holding Mike's hand, she felt him tap out a rhythm against her wrist. The tune rang in her heart, knowing that the two of them would have this harmony for the rest of their lives.

. . .

Don't miss the next book in the Honor Valley
Holiday series!

*He's all about discipline, she's all about dessert, and
their worlds are about to collide in the most delicious
way.*

Holly Evergreen is excited to take on the mission to
spread holiday cheer by preparing a meal especially
for the children on base. Christmas is her favorite
time of the year, and as a pastry chef she's thrilled to
make sweet treats for the kids in the community
whose families sacrifice the most. But when her
older brother's best friend is announced as the chef
for the adults, the sparks that fly just might burn
down the kitchen.

Ryan, regimented and health-conscious, takes one
look at Holly's sugar-laden Christmas menu and
decides it needs an overhaul. Holly, however,

believes that the joy of the season comes sprinkled with sugar and a dollop of whipped cream. With the big holiday dinner drawing near, the two clash and sizzle, discovering that their differences might just be the ingredients for a love they never saw coming.

Can Holly make Ryan see the sweeter side of life? Find out in this holiday romance that weaves together an older hero, his best friend's all grown up sister, a little sugar and spice, and the spirit of the holidays.

Love in a Decked Hall is a part of the Honor Valley Holiday romances; a heartwarming, small town, military romance series that explores the power of love, growth, and healing set during the most magical time of the year! These stories are short and sweet -the perfect length for an afternoon pick me up or an evening escape before bedtime!

SHANAE JOHNSON

Love in a
Decked Hall

HONOR VALLEY HOLIDAYS

CHAPTER ONE

The air in Holly Evergreen's kitchen was thick with the scents of cinnamon, vanilla, and melting chocolate—a heavenly tapestry of aromas that hung in the air. Holly's focus was singular: perfecting the quintessential Christmas cookie. The baked good was a creation meant to offer a warm hug and a whispered assurance that everything would be okay during the most wonderful time of the year.

Holly's fingers sifted through flour, soft and powdery like the season's first snowfall. The dough beneath her hands was supple, a blank canvas begging for artistic touch. Glancing at her reflection in the oven's glass door, she saw her plump, plus-sized figure and smiled. She was the kind of woman a young, jolly Santa would adore. In a world that often prized stick figures, Holly was unabashedly herself—full of love, full of life, and full of the spirit of Christmas.

The upcoming holiday dinner at the military base was both her mission and her challenge. The menu she was crafting was more than a list of dishes. It was an anthology of love notes, all written in the universal language of sugar and spice.

These desserts weren't mere treats. They were messages to the kids on the base. *You're loved. You're special. This Christmas, you won't be alone.*

Even though that last message wasn't necessarily true. Many of the kids would be alone. Children of military families made just a great a sacrifice as their parents, often going without their parents' presence on birthdays, school events, and holidays.

"Holly, these cookies look divine, as always. But are you sure about the triple chocolate chunk?"

Holly wrinkled her nose at her cousin Felice as though she'd said the most ridiculous thing in the world. "Christmas without chocolate is like Santa without his reindeer—simply incomplete and wholly unimaginable." With a smile, she pressed a chunk of chocolate into the dough.

Joy, her other favorite cousin, piped in from her

place at the kitchen table where she was cataloguing kids' letters to Santa. "You know the dinner at the base is a big deal. Make sure you're preparing for all kinds of tastes, not just those who appreciate a sugar rush."

The caution in Joy's voice stirred a fleeting unease within Holly. She knew the world was full of people who viewed her craft—her passion—as trivial or indulgent. But to her, each sugary creation was a vessel of joy, a talisman against life's cold realities. She believed in the transformative power of her sweets, their ability to turn any frown into a smile, any evening into a celebration.

Holly took a deep breath, inhaling the mingling scents of sugar and spice that filled her little corner of the world. Tonight, as she planned the menu for the holiday dinner, she would infuse it with her philosophy—that love, like baking, was a generous act. She held on to the hope that her creations would not only fill plates but also warm hearts, turning this Christmas into a season where joy was the greatest gift of all.

She would be testing this recipe out tomorrow at the family cooking class she hosted each month on the base. As she slid the cookie tray into the oven, Holly wished not for a perfect cookie, but for a perfect moment—when the military families would bite into her creations and taste the love and warmth she baked into every morsel. As the oven's heat began to rise, so too did her hopes for the coming holiday season.

Felice began a rousing rendition of "Jingle Bells" as she went over the list of songs she planned for the choir. Felice was in charge of the Christmas carol concert this year. Joy was in charge of the toy drive. The Evergreen family had pretty much been predisposed to love the winter holidays, so it was no surprise that each of the girls took up extra duties during the season.

"How's carol practice going?" Holly asked Felice.

Her cousin's eyes were as bright as tinsel as she answered. "Everything's falling into place, but we still need a baritone. Know anyone?"

Holly took a thoughtful sip of her peppermint mocha, her mind flipping through a mental Rolodex. "Hmm, a baritone. Let me think on it. You never know who might walk into the bakery one of these days."

"Right, between your cookies and my choir, we could practically build a gingerbread chapel."

"That'll be Ginger's job," said Felice. "You know her mom's looking to retire, and Ginger's hoping to be put in charge of the gingerbread house competition this year."

"Looks like the new generation of Evergreens are all taking the reins."

"You guys, I'm having the hardest time with finding gifts for the toy drive." Joy, who'd been quiet, suddenly sighed, disrupting the light-hearted banter.

"Is this the Star Voyager toy?" asked Holly.

"It's the one toy that every child on the planet seems to want this Christmas. I've checked everywhere, and it's sold out."

Holly's heart constricted at her cousin's plight. "Oh, Joy, that's really tough. But if anyone can make that Christmas wish come true, it's you."

Felice nodded in agreement. "Absolutely. Between the three of us, we'll find that toy and give that kid a Christmas to remember."

And there it was, that resilient spirit of Christmas, refusing to be dampened by any hurdle. Holly looked at her cousins, their faces illuminated by the soft glow of the string lights hanging from her kitchen window. Each of them, in their own way, was a Christmas warrior, fighting to make the holiday season a little brighter, a little merrier.

"I know things seem stressful now," Holly began, leaning in closer, "but when we look back, we won't remember the stress or the hurdles. We'll remember the smiles, the thank-yous, and the looks on people's faces when we give them a reason to celebrate."

Both Felice and Joy nodded, their faces softening.

"This is what we Evergreens do, right?" Holly continued. "We make Christmas miracles happen. Felice will find her baritone. Joy will get that Star Voyager toy. And my holiday dinner at the base is going to be the best those kids ever had."

The three women clinked their coffee mugs together, making a sacred pact sealed with caffeine and Christmas spirit.

"Here's to the best Christmas ever," Felice declared.

"Yes," Joy added, "the very best."

Feeling invigorated, Holly sipped her peppermint mocha. As the warm liquid met her lips, she thought of all the faces that would light up this Christmas— thanks to a carol, a toy, or even a cookie. And in that moment, the weight of her responsibilities felt lighter, like the first snowflake of winter, delicate but filled with endless possibilities.

CHAPTER TWO

The air inside Ryan's modest living room was thick with the smell of fresh pine, emanating from a Christmas tree that was more ornament than tree. Red and gold baubles clung to every branch, twinkling mockingly as if they knew he was out of his element. His mother-in-law, Janice, prattled on about routines, bedtimes, and preferred cereal brands. All Ryan heard was the relentless ticking of the wall clock, counting down to his new life as a solo parent.

"Remember, Rose likes her peanut butter sandwiches without the crust. Lily will only eat cornflakes. No bran flakes, heaven forbid." Janice's words were tinged with a humor Ryan didn't quite share at the moment.

"Crustless sandwiches and cornflakes. Anything else?" His voice carried a note of bravado he didn't feel.

Janice peered at him, her eyes softening. "You'll be fine, Ryan. Just remember, they're little girls, not recruits. Ease up on the drill sergeant act."

"Don't worry, I won't have them doing push-ups if they don't finish their vegetables." He chuckled, more out of nervousness than amusement.

Whatever the sound was, it was good enough for Janice. She gave a satisfied bob of her head and picked up her travel bag. She paused at the door to give him a reassuring hug. "I'll be back before New Year's. Just a little cruise to get away for a while. Call if you need anything."

The door clicked shut behind her. Ryan was left standing in the deafening silence of his own home. He looked around at the walls adorned with family photos, at the Christmas tree that seemed almost out of place now, and then at his two little girls—Rose, six, and Lily, four—both eyeing him with a mix of curiosity and doubt.

For a man who'd led troops, who'd executed intricate drills and maneuvers, he suddenly felt ill-equipped and, dare he say, terrified. The military had trained him for many things. It had not prepared him for the challenge now sitting on his own living room rug, expectantly staring up at him.

Rose broke the silence. "Daddy, I want a snack."

It was a simple request, yet it sent Ryan's mind spiraling.

Bran flakes? No.

Crustless sandwiches. Right.

He moved toward the kitchen. His normally confident steps were replaced by a hesitant shuffle. As he stood before the open fridge, he realized he was in uncharted territory. For nearly his whole military career, he'd mostly existed on MREs. Those meals ready to eat were not the tastiest foods out there, but they gave a soldier everything necessary to complete a mission.

What was inside his fridge were a number of things ready to eat right out of the package. Frozen chicken nuggets. Frozen pizzas. Pop-Tarts.

What was in the cabinets was no better. Sugary cereal. Highly processed treats. Sodium packed crackers.

One of the things that had excited Ryan the most about coming home was the abundance of fresh foods that would be at his disposal. Peanut butter wasn't a bad choice. It wasn't the best choice either.

The preservative-laden jelly was simply out of the question.

But this battle was neither here nor there. Because it wasn't dinner time. The clock on the wall read 3 p.m. The military clock Ryan had abided by for years said that dinner was at 17:30 hours.

"No snacks before dinner," he said, maintaining his drill sergeant tone. "It's unhealthy."

Both girls erupted into wails that would put any morning reveille to shame. As their cries escalated, Ryan felt a headache brewing like an incoming storm. He relented. "Fine. But it's going to be a healthy snack."

Returning from the kitchen, he offered a plate filled with carrot sticks and a bowl of hummus. "Eat up."

Rose poked at a carrot with disdain. "This isn't a snack, Daddy. It's a punishment."

Before Ryan could marshal a response, the doorbell rang, rescuing him from the impending mutiny. He opened the door to find Lucas, his old army buddy, standing there with a grin.

"Hey, man! Long time no see." Lucas pulled him into a quick, back-thumping hug.

"You're telling me," Ryan sighed. "Come in. But fair warning, I'm navigating a dietary rebellion here."

Lucas chuckled as he stepped inside, his eyes quickly noting the untouched carrots and hummus. "Tough crowd, huh? Look, I've got just the thing. There's a cooking class for kids and parents tomorrow on the base. I'm taking my niece and nephew. Why don't you come along? It might be fun. Lord knows you could use all the help you can get."

A cooking class seemed so foreign to him, so… undisciplined. Yet he considered the untouched carrots, his daughters' forlorn faces, and his own floundering attempts at home life. Maybe this was exactly what they needed—a little culinary anarchy to shake up their rigid routine.

"You know what? We'll be there," Ryan finally said.

"Great." Lucas slapped him on the back. "Trust me, it's going to be fun."

As Lucas left, Ryan looked at his daughters, who were now curiously eyeing him. Maybe, just maybe, this cooking class would be the olive branch he needed to mend his faltering rapport with his girls.

"All right, girls, how about we try something new tomorrow?" Ryan suggested, trying to inject some excitement into his voice.

"What's that, Daddy?" Rose asked, her curiosity overcoming her earlier defiance.

"We're going to a cooking class. How does that sound?"

Both girls exchanged a glance before breaking into smiles. It was a small win, but right now, Ryan would take any victory he could get. As he scraped the carrots and hummus back into their respective containers, he allowed himself to entertain the notion that there might be more than one way to run a household, and more than one way to be a good father.

CHAPTER THREE

*H*oliday spirit was rife in the mess hall of the Honor Valley military base. Tables dressed in red and green were neatly lined up, each bearing a delightful assortment of cookie cutters, sugar sprinkles, and dollops of icing. The air tingled with the scent of sugar cookies and ginger-bread, blending seamlessly with the cheerful hum of Christmas carols piped through the speakers.

Holly tightened the red ribbon in her wavy brown hair. Here, in this kingdom of confectionery, she felt most alive. Her eyes gleamed as she prepared to demonstrate the delicate art of glazing a ginger-bread man when a disturbance rose from the back of the room. A tall, impeccably fit man stood there, embroiled in a passionate disagreement with two little girls.

"No extra sugar on the cookies. Sugar is basically poison, you know."

"But Daddy, it's Christmas," one of the girls wailed, her little hands forming into frustrated fists.

Abandoning her unglazed gingerbread men, Holly approached the trio, her red flats lightly tapping on the floor. "I couldn't help but overhear. Christmas just isn't the same without a little sugar and spice. Even Santa would tell you that."

The man's intense eyes—pools of blue-gray—moved to her. For a moment, Holly felt a rush of déjà vu. There was something vaguely familiar about him, a ghostly echo from her past. He regarded her as if she were a stranger. An intrusive, unwelcome stranger, at that. Even though she'd been leading the class for the last twenty minutes.

"Santa isn't the epitome of health, now is he?" There wasn't even a hint of humor softening his words. "I prefer not to take nutritional advice from a fictional character."

"Oh, come on. Even Scrooge allowed himself a feast. It's about the joy and the memories, not a life-time of dietary choices."

He sighed, clearly unswayed. "Respectfully, I have to disagree."

It was then that it hit her—those eyes, that voice. This was Ryan Blake, her older brother's best friend, the man she'd been infatuated with since her teenage years. The weight of years and unspoken feelings pressed heavily on her, mingled with the sweetness of the air.

He looked very much changed. Even older than the eight-year difference between them. Through Holly's eyes, Ryan was almost a stranger, a poignant contrast to the boyish charm he used to wear like a second skin. He stood there, his back as rigid as a flagpole, shoulders broader, arms more defined. His military service had sculpted him, but not in the way an artist brings life to clay. No, it was as if life had chipped away at him, hardening him into a stoic statue.

She'd stopped daydreaming about him so much after learning he'd gotten married. His wife and family had lived on bases across the states for a time. And then Holly had heard of Christine's untimely death a few years ago.

Her eyes hesitated on Ryan's face, searching for remnants of the past. But the softness that had once lived in his cheeks was gone, replaced by angles and lines carved from duty and, perhaps, suffering. His jaw was set, clenched like a locked gate guarding a long-abandoned house. The lips that had once curved so easily into a smile, the smile that could disarm anyone—her especially—now lay in a straight, unyielding line.

His eyes, once brimming with mirth and youthful recklessness, seemed to have absorbed the world's weight. A penetrating gaze that used to sparkle with mischief now held an intensity she couldn't place; it was as if they had turned into fortified walls. The warmth she remembered was replaced by a glint of steel, a barrier against vulnerabilities.

It unnerved her, this transformation. What had carved him into this? And yet, amid this constellation of changes, there was still something—some essence of him—that tugged at her memory and her heart. For better or worse, he had changed, but then again, so had she.

He looked at his daughters, their little faces the epitome of disappointment. "Fine, but just a little," he finally conceded, and the girls erupted in glee, rushing toward the sprinkle jars as if they contained the secrets of the universe.

As Holly watched the girls dash off, her emotions

swirled like the colors in a candy cane. Here was Ryan, as solid and real as ever but seemingly indifferent to her presence. Could her gingerbread men and sugary dreams weave a hint of magic into this renewed acquaintance?

"You're in charge here?" he asked, his eyes scanning the room, never quite meeting hers.

"Yes," Holly said, her voice tinged with a wistfulness she hoped he wouldn't detect. "I like to think I'm Santa's little helper, spreading joy one cookie at a time."

His lips tightened as he examined the sugary concoction. "You know, you could easily make these cookies healthier. Ever tried a quinoa or almond base? Less sugar, perhaps?"

Holly blinked, surprised at his audacity to critique her prized recipes. "Healthy is a smoothie in the morning. But this"—she waved her hand over the plate—"this is Christmas. It's about indulgence, joy, and memories that last a lifetime."

Ryan arched an eyebrow, clearly unimpressed. "I think you can have all of those without clogging your arteries."

"Maybe so, but sometimes, the heart needs what the heart needs. Even if that's a little sugar."

"Or a lot of sugar, judging by this spread." Ryan's

eyes scanned the festive table as if he were evaluating a military operation. "Look, I get that people enjoy treats, but as someone organizing this event, you have a responsibility. Why not teach these kids that they can have fun while eating well?"

Holly sighed, a tinge of exasperation flavoring her emotions. She took in his earnest face and rigid stance. This was not the Ryan Blake of her youthful dreams—the carefree guy who used to sneak her cookies from the top shelf. The man before her seemed as flexible as a candy cane, straight and unbending.

"I do teach responsibility, in moderation. But this is the season of giving, of dreaming, of believing in a bit of magic. And sometimes, magic tastes like sugar cookies and peppermint bark."

His jaw tightened, and Holly could tell she'd struck a chord, albeit a dissonant one. He looked as though he was about to counter, but Holly didn't give him the chance. She placed a gingerbread cookie into his hand. He looked down at it in shock, as though he expected the sugar to leap up and assault him.

"If you'll excuse me," she said, lifting her chin, "I have cookies to decorate and joy to spread." She turned and walked away, her red flats echoing softly against the floor.

Ryan Blake could be a grinch all he wanted. She had an army of gingerbread men to bring to life, and they, at least, would be as sweet as she believed Christmas should be.

CHAPTER FOUR

*A*midst the din of joyful holiday chatter and the scent of cinnamon and vanilla wafting through the air, Ryan surveyed the hall. The woman at the front, handling cookie dough with the grace of a seasoned chef, had caught his attention. There was a softness about her, a vitality that was as infectious as it was intriguing. Curves in all the right places, like the perfect Christmas pastry—full and satisfying. He felt a flicker of something he hadn't felt in years: desire.

"Man, she's something else, isn't she?" Lucas came up beside him. "I still remember the apple turnovers she made for the junior bake sale."

Ryan's eyes remained fixed on her. "She seems familiar."

"Yeah, that's Holly Evergreen."

Evergreen? Suddenly, it hit him like a snowball to the face. Garland's little sister. Ryan felt as though the floor had just dropped out from under him.

"Wait. That's little Holly Evergreen?"

"The one and only," Lucas confirmed. "Not so little anymore, though I keep forgetting you're older than me."

Ryan's gut tightened. Oh no, this was bad. This was against the code, the guy code, the soldier code. It went against every code he knew. She was younger, far younger, and his best friend's sister. A boundary one simply didn't cross. Garland would probably strangle him with a string of Christmas lights.

Still, Ryan couldn't stop his eyes from straying to Holly again. She was laughing at something a little boy said. Her eyes twinkled as she bent down to the kid's level and handed him a sugar cookie. Ryan couldn't decide if he wanted to snatch the cookie out of her hand or snatch her to him.

For a moment, Ryan let himself wonder what it would be like to let go, to taste the sweetness that life had to offer, to feel something beyond the rigidity and routine he had confined himself to.

No. He shook his head mentally. That door had

closed the moment he heard the name Evergreen. It was better that way—simpler. He'd spent the past two years building walls around himself, around his heart, like a fortress, to keep out anything that might disrupt his life further.

Ryan wasn't sure he'd been the best husband to Christine. He'd been a good provider, but he hadn't been there for his wife. Not even when she'd died.

Two years had passed since his wife's death, and while time had muddled the sharp edges of his grief, it hadn't softened the fortress around his heart. No, that fortress had only thickened. Each layer was a defensive response to his own failings as a husband. He'd provided for his family, sure. A nice home, food on the table, a secure future for his daughters. But what about the emotional sustenance his wife had needed?

The memories, like specters, floated in the peripheries of his mind. How many times had he opted for another deployment rather than facing the emotional labor required at home? How many times had he decided that his role was merely that of a provider, neglecting the lover, the partner, the confidant he had vowed to be?

And when she had needed him the most, at her most vulnerable, he hadn't been there. His absence at her deathbed, something he couldn't blame on deployment or duty, was the cornerstone of his fortress—a heavy stone he carried in the pockets of his soul.

Now as he leaned against the wall, he contemplated the life he was trying to reconstruct. For the first time in years, someone had made him wonder if the fortress could have windows, cracks through which light could seep. Little Holly Evergreen had exposed a weakness and made him question if he wanted to spend the rest of his life encased in this self-imposed exile.

With a heavy sigh, Ryan realized that the ultimate act of courage wouldn't be to strengthen the fortress, but to allow someone to breach it. It scared him, the idea of relinquishing control, of tearing down walls brick by emotional brick. Yet the alternative—a life devoid of love, of touch, of shared laughter and tears —seemed far more terrifying.

But that someone could not be his best friend's little sister, no matter how delectable a mouth-watering treat she appeared to be.

The workshop was coming to an end, and Ryan found himself wrestling with more than just the culinary dilemma before him. He stared at the cookie—Holly's cookie—in his hand. It was a gingerbread man, smothered in rich icing and dotted with sugar buttons, a sugary embodiment of everything he'd sworn off but was strangely tempted by now.

His gaze darted toward Holly. She was engaged in a lively conversation with a parent, laughing at something said. Her laughter was like the tinkling of Christmas bells—joyful, infectious. She was a living, breathing holiday spirit, and the contradiction of it all pricked at him. He had decided it was time to get back into the dating scene, to find a stable step-mother for his girls, and Holly was absolutely not what he had in mind.

"She's just too young, too... indulgent," he muttered under his breath.

"What was that?" Lucas glanced his way.

"Nothing." Ryan brushed it off. "Just thinking."

He raised the cookie to his mouth, a fort of self-imposed restrictions trembling on the brink of collapse. With a resigned sigh, he took a bite.

Oh, Holy Mother of Mercy, was it good.

No, not good. The cookie was a revelation. The spices of ginger and cinnamon, happiness and light had been distilled into this one bite. He couldn't help the deep, visceral moan that escaped his lips.

Holly turned just in time, locking eyes with him. Her lips curved into a self-satisfied, *I-told-you-so* smile, and he felt simultaneously caught and enchanted.

"See? Not bad, huh?" Lucas nudged him.

"Exceptionally bad for my regimen," Ryan said, but the words lacked conviction.

For a moment, the room, with its festivity and cacophony of joy, seemed to fade away. It was just Holly's eyes on him—those beautiful eyes, sparkling with triumph and something softer. Something he couldn't place but felt drawn to.

Holly Evergreen was totally wrong for him. Every rational fiber in his being knew that. Yet as he took another bite, finishing off the gingerbread man in two guilty but delightful bites, Ryan felt a different sort of hunger awaken. A hunger for something more unpredictable, something sweet, something like the woman smiling across the room.

CHAPTER FIVE

"*L*ooks fantastic, Holly. You've really outdone yourself this year." Commander Mitchell nodded, flipping through the report.

"Thank you, Commander. The holidays are special for everyone, but I think they're even more so for our families here." Holly felt a warm flush of pride as she finished presenting her holiday plans to the base committee.

As the committee members murmured their agreement, Holly let herself relish the moment. The room was bright, flooded with the winter sunlight pouring through the tall windows. She could hear the distant hum of activity from the base outside.

Then the door creaked open, and he walked in—

Ryan Blake, in all his broad-shouldered, squared-jawed glory.

Holly's stomach did a little flip as she watched him move with the assured gait of a man who knew his place in the world. Yet when he took a seat and glanced through the menu she had carefully curated, his eyebrows knitted together in what could only be described as disapproval.

"I have some concerns about the menu." Ryan spoke, finally, looking straight at Commander Mitchell but completely ignoring her.

It was as if their cookie encounter last night had never happened. As if the years of him coming into her back door to snag treats from her mother's pantry had never taken place.

"Go on." The commander nodded.

"As we all know, childhood obesity is a concern. I'd suggest we consider a healthier menu," Ryan began, his voice carrying that annoying tone of paternalistic wisdom. "Perhaps replacing the sugar cookies with a fruit platter and the chocolate mousse with yogurt parfaits?"

Holly couldn't believe it. The gall of the man. As if Christmas could ever be complete without the rich sweetness of cocoa, the heavenly aroma of cinnamon, or the joyful crunch of a well-baked sugar cookie.

"Christmas is about tradition, joy, and yes, indulgence," she found herself saying, her voice laced with an emotional cocktail of irritation and incredulity. "The occasional sweet treat never hurt anyone."

"But is indulgence what we need to promote?" Ryan's gaze finally met hers for the first time.

For a moment, their eyes locked, and Holly felt like they were the only two people in the room. A flurry of emotions stormed through her. She was furious, yes. But also unsettlingly aware of how attractive he looked. Especially when he was all fired up.

It was confusing. It was thrilling. It was aggravating.

Holly regained her composure and turned back to the commander. He was much easier to address than the soldier drilling her with that unwavering gaze. "Christmas is once a year. If we can't let ourselves enjoy a sugar cookie during the holidays, then when can we? The dinner should remind the kids of family and fun, of warmth and of simpler times. Taking that away would be like ripping the soul out of Christmas."

The room went quiet. The tension in the air

hung"so thick Holly felt she could slice it with her dullest knife. The committee room felt like a battleground, one where Holly was willing to defend her sugar cookies to the last crumb.

"Holly has a point," said the commander. "Christmas without cookies is frankly un-American."

The committee nodded in agreement, and Holly felt a rush of triumphant relief. But as she looked at Ryan, who was clearly frustrated but oddly more intriguing than ever, she wondered if this was just the first of many battles to come. And for reasons she didn't fully understand, that thought was as frightening as it was electrifying.

"When it comes to the menu, it's not just about sugar cookies," Ryan argued, his eyes capturing hers with the intensity of a laser. "We should be teaching kids the value of good nutrition, even during the holidays."

"Excuse me, but it's Christmas, not a nutrition class," she shot back.

"Christmas is a season for adults, too. And it's time we grow up and accept that things can't always be candy canes and sugarplums."

Just as Holly was about to unleash a well-crafted rebuttal, Commander Mitchell interrupted.

"Enough, you two. We're here to plan a holiday event, not ignite World War III. Holly, Ryan, I propose a compromise. Why don't the two of you work together to create a balanced menu?"

Holly felt her mouth drop open in disbelief. Work with Ryan? Was the commander joking?

"Sir, with all due respect, I think—"

Commander Mitchell held up his hand, silencing whatever Ryan was about to say. "In the spirit of collaboration and holiday cheer, let's give this a shot. Holly, you can visit Ryan's home to try out some recipes. Maybe you'll find a middle ground."

Suddenly, the room was abuzz with the clatter of chairs and the shuffling of papers. The people were clearly done with this topic and ready to move on with their agenda. The room emptied quickly, leaving only Holly and Ryan.

Ryan looked just as surprised as she felt, but she noticed the slightest quiver in his lips, as though he were suppressing a smile. Was he laughing at her? That was the final straw.

"Fine," Holly finally muttered, gathering her papers into a neat pile. "I'll bring the sugar, you bring your...kale. Let's see what kind of Christmas miracle we can whip up."

As Holly left the room, her emotions were a

swirling snowstorm of frustration, indignation, and —she had to admit—a certain exhilarating sense of challenge. Ryan Blake was not the man she'd daydreamed about in her younger years. He was rigid, argumentative, and far too serious.

And he still didn't remember her.

CHAPTER SIX

*T*he atmosphere in Ryan's living room was a battlefield of toys, crayon sketches, and abandoned hair ties. It was carnage that even his drill sergeant instincts hadn't prepared him for. His nostrils flared at the incongruent mix of scented candles he'd lit in an attempt to conjure some sort of domestic tranquility.

"All right, girls, time to clean up this mess. Operation Toy Tidy begins now. On the double," Ryan barked, his voice echoing with a military precision that had once commanded rows of recruits.

Emily, the eldest, stared up at him, her eyes wide, holding her doll like a protective shield. His youngest, Rose, simply plopped herself down amidst the chaos, defiantly continuing to color outside the lines of her coloring book.

Ryan's molars ground behind his pursed lips. This was supposed to be easy. He was trained to handle conflict, to defuse ticking time bombs. And yet his daughters' resistance was disarming him in a way he had never experienced.

His phone buzzed on the coffee table. When he glanced at the caller ID, he unclenched his teeth and grabbed for the device like a lifeline.

"Janice, are you there?"

"Can you believe I can get reception out in the middle of the ocean?"

Ryan held the phone away from his mouth to let the weary sigh go past the receiver.

"We are having a lovely time. George and I will definitely bring the girls next time. There's so much to do onboard."

Ryan only barely kept himself from asking exactly when they'd plan that trip. It couldn't come soon enough. But by then, his girls would likely be feral and starved.

"How's it going, Ryan?"

"Everything's great, just great," he lied, his eyes darting across the room as if searching for an escape route. "We're all getting along like peas in a pod."

Emily knocked over a glass of juice, the orange liquid pooling like a splash of defeat on his hardwood floor. "Uh oh, spaghetti-o's."

Janice's laughter trickled through the phone. "Sounds like Emily just had an accident."

The doorbell rang, mercifully cutting the conversation short. "Hey, Janice, someone's at the door. I'll catch up with you later."

"You do that, Ryan. And remember, they're just kids. You'll figure it out."

Just kids. A concept he was grappling to understand in a home that felt less like a sanctuary and more like a war zone. He hung up and made his way to the door, his feet heavier with each step. His palm hovered over the knob for a half-second, as if cautioning himself, before turning it and pulling the door open.

And there she was. Holly. Dressed in a Christmas sweater adorned with gleaming reindeer and snowflakes. Her leggings hugged her curves in a way that made his pulse quicken for the wrong—no, inappropriate—reasons. Her hair was a cascade of dark locks that framed her face like a halo. And her eyes—those bright eyes—twinkled with a joy that seemed intrinsically tied to the season.

"Mr. Blake."

"Holly Berry."

She prickled at the old nickname, just like the leaves of the bush she was named for. "You remember me?"

"Of course, I remember you." His voice was deliberately flat, devoid of the warmth that her appearance tempted out of him. It was as though a rigid wall had sprung up inside him, and he was determined to let no emotion, no attraction breach it.

As Holly stepped in, her boots left a pattern of melted snowflakes on the doormat. She looked around, soaking in the lived-in chaos of his life. He inhaled deeply, trying not to breathe in the floral perfume she wore, which mixed absurdly well with the aroma of cinnamon-scented candles he'd lit in another ill-fated attempt at domestic tranquility.

This was Garland's little sister, he reminded himself. Any more thoughts along those romantic lines would be a one-way ticket to disaster.

"How's Garland?" Ryan asked.

"He's fine. He got leave for Christmas. So he should be home soon."

The pitter-patter of tiny feet drew his attention back to the family room as Emily and Rose scampered into the foyer. Without hesitation, they wrapped their arms around Holly, their faces bright-ening like Christmas lights.

"Miss Holly," they chimed in unison.

The knot in Ryan's stomach tightened. They'd met Holly for all of a single cooking class. Yet here they were, embracing her like a long-lost family member.

With maternal grace, Holly bent down to their level, her eyes twinkling as she returned their hugs. "Hey, you two."

"Are you here to cook?"

"Can we help?"

"You sure can," said Holly. "I'm going to give the two of you the most important job in the kitchen. That's clean-up. You can't make yummy food in a messy kitchen. Got it?"

"Got it," the girls said in unison.

To Ryan's disbelief, his daughters listened. They listened and obeyed without a single whine or complaint. Emily went to the sink to grab a dish towel and began sopping up the orange juice. Rose began putting the dirty dishes into the dishwasher as though she'd done it before a million times.

"Seems like you have a way with kids," he said.

"Or maybe kids just have a way of knowing who they can trust," she retorted lightly, her words punctuated by a smile that made his traitorous heart skip a beat.

There was so much he wanted to say, so much he wanted to feel but shouldn't. His emotions were a battlefield, his desires the enemy combatants he had to subdue.

"Shall we get started on this cooking experiment?" he asked, redirecting the conversation away from the dangerous territory it was veering toward.

"After you," Holly said, motioning toward the kitchen.

As he led her in that direction, Ryan couldn't shake the nagging feeling that the walls he'd so carefully constructed were starting to crack, and he was utterly unprepared for whatever lay on the other side.

CHAPTER SEVEN

*a*s Holly stepped into Ryan's kitchen, she was immediately aware of how the space seemed to shrink with him in it. Not because it was small. Because his presence was like a gravitational field, pulling her focus, her senses, all onto him. The scent of basil and thyme filled the air, but it was the undercurrent of his cologne—earthy, masculine—that tickled her senses and made her pulse accelerate.

Clad in a fitted T-shirt that highlighted the contours of his muscles, Ryan moved with the kind of confidence she'd always admired, and maybe even fantasized about. She watched as he measured out grains in a cup, his fingers sure and his movements crisp, his biceps subtly flexing with each motion.

Holly found herself wondering what those hands, that strength, would feel like against her skin.

Snap out of it, Holly!

"It's important for kids to learn about flavors," she said, purposefully steering her thoughts back to safer ground. "Don't you think?"

Ryan's kids were seated in the other room with peanut butter and jam roll-ups. It was a quick and easy treat that Holly had carried in her back pocket ever since she was a babysitter. She'd have the kids roll out the bread with a rolling pin. Then spread the peanut butter and jam on the flattened bread. Though Ryan had insisted on sugar-free jelly.

Really, who does that?

The girls hadn't minded. Or they hadn't noticed. After they'd rolled up the treats and cut them with a butter knife in sections, they delightedly tossed them in their mouths while sitting in front of the television.

"Flavors, sure," Ryan responded, casting a dubious glance at the sugar canister on the counter. "But not every flavor has to be sweet."

Holly stirred the mixture in front of her, taking in the medley of colors: the vivid red of the apple, the earthy brown of the cinnamon, and the golden glow of butter. Yet despite the aesthetic beauty, it was the momentary flicker of Ryan's gaze to his daughters that struck her the most.

Each time he looked their way, his eyes softened with a mixture of love and a hint of uncertainty, as if the very act of caring for them was both his anchor and his uncharted sea. That vulnerability—so at odds with his strong exterior—tugged at Holly's heartstrings, making her fall just a smidgen more in love with him.

Then the moment shattered.

"Holly, do we really need all this sugar?" Ryan held the canister as if it were an illicit substance.

"It's Christmas, Ryan. It's literally the season of sweetness," she argued, her fingers gripping the wooden spoon a little too tightly.

"I just think we can do without—"

"Without joy? Without tradition?" she found herself saying, the words spilling out before she could rein them in. "Look, I get that you want your girls to eat healthy, but there's a time and a place for indulgence. It's not just about the sugar. It's about the experience, the memories you make while enjoying something sweet and homey."

He stared at her, his gaze intense, searching. For a moment, Holly thought she saw something there—understanding, maybe even desire. But it vanished almost as quickly as it had appeared, leaving her in a sea of emotional disarray.

"Fine. You do it your way," he said finally, his voice softer as he put the sugar canister back on the counter. "I'll do mine my way."

The room fell quiet except for the subtle sounds of cooking—the sizzle of butter in the pan, the chop of the knife through berries. Holly allowed herself one last stolen glance at Ryan, watching as he bit his lower lip, deep in thought.

She picked up a small piece of apple with her fingers, sugared and soft, still warm from the pan. "Try this."

Ryan hesitated for a split second before leaning forward. As his lips closed over her fingertips to accept the bite, they brushed against her skin. A shiver raced down her spine, leaving a tingling sensation in its wake. Her mind wandered briefly to what those lips would feel like on hers. Soft yet assertive? A curious blend of sweet and savory?

"How is it?" Holly managed to ask.

"Good," he said, pausing as if considering his next words. "Really good, actually."

A thrill of delight surged through her at his admission, but before she could fully savor the moment, Ryan picked up a spoon and scooped a small amount of his own creation—a quinoa and berry mixture with a hint of mint. "Your turn," he said, offering the spoon to her lips.

She opened her mouth, letting him feed her. The instant the flavors hit her tongue, she couldn't help but feel surprised. It was good—surprisingly good—even with the healthy sugar alternative he'd used. Sweet, but not overpoweringly so, and balanced by the tartness of the berries and the cool edge of mint.

"So?" Ryan raised an eyebrow.

"It's good," she admitted, trying to mask how much she really liked it.

His grin widened at her reluctant admission, but before either of them could say another word, something inexplicable took hold of her. Maybe it was the sweetness of the moment, the blend of culinary victories on both their parts, or perhaps it was the accumulation of years of hidden emotions and suppressed desires. Whatever it was, Holly suddenly found herself rising onto her tiptoes.

She kissed him.

The contact was unlike anything she'd fantasized. Instead of the warm, magnetic pull she'd imagined, there was a stiffness, an unexpected rigidity to Ryan's lips. For a disconcerting second, he didn't respond. His lips firmed into a line that didn't part, didn't curve, didn't move.

The awkwardness hovered in that interminable second, stretching it out like a taut rubber band on the verge of snapping. A flood of panic seeped into the fringes of Holly's mind. Had she misread the signals? God, was she about to become a cautionary tale, a cringeworthy anecdote shared over beer and nachos?

Then she felt it—the tiniest change. A subtle shift in his posture, the faintest softening of his lips. But the moment was like an awkwardly timed dance move, slightly off-beat, leaving both dancers unsure of the next step.

When they finally pulled apart, Holly was mortified and confused. His eyes met hers, and in them, she saw a war of conflicting emotions, almost as if he were as baffled by their lip-lock fiasco as she was. She couldn't help the disappointment coursing through her. That kiss was a far cry from the romantic moment she'd built up in her head over the years. And now she could never take it back.

CHAPTER EIGHT

*R*yan thought he was standing in his kitchen, but right now, it felt like a whole different realm. It was as if he had stepped out of his own body and was watching a scene unfold from a distance, like an audience member in a movie theater.

The laughter and chatter from the cartoon his daughters were engrossed in drifted from the family room, punctuating the air with innocence and child-like wonder. His senses were overwhelmingly, tanta-lizingly alive. The lingering taste of sugar from Holly's apple dish still coated his tongue, making him momentarily question his sworn allegiance against it. The flavor of mint and berries from his dish mingled in, adding complexity to the sensory experience.

Yet what left him utterly confounded was an indescribable taste that he knew was pure Holly. It was a taste that no Michelin-star chef could replicate. It was a taste that no exotic spice could mimic. It was an intoxicating blend of her essence, her aroma, and her spirit. And just like that, he felt his fortress not just breached, but shattered.

"You kissed me," he found himself saying, as if stating the obvious would somehow rewrite the awkwardness out of the moment.

"Yeah," she sighed, her voice tinged with unmistakable disappointment.

That sigh traveled straight to his gut, twisting it into knots.

Ryan was still reeling from the unexpected contact of Holly's lips, the bewildering and strangely disappointing execution of it all. Her frown, a tiny contraction of her brows and a downturn of her lovely mouth, was like a pinprick to his ego.

"I was surprised." He fumbled with his words. "You caught me off guard."

"Well, now I know and can let go of this crush I've had for years." She shrugged, a lift of her shoulders that scrunched up her features. Then her shoulders fell.

Ryan felt the drop in his stomach.

Crush? For years? That revelation stunned him even more than the kiss had. The air between them thickened. Every atom vibrated with a tension that was as unbearable as it was electric.

Ryan felt a rush of something intense and irrational. Defiance? Desire? Call it what you will, but it yanked him out of his stupor.

"I know how to kiss a woman," he declared, his voice almost a growl.

Again, she simply shrugged. But this time, before her shoulders dropped, Ryan reached for her. He stopped the downward motion with a hand on each of her forearms.

In a bold move, one that shoved aside every doubt and reason for hesitation, he pulled her close. His hands found the small of her back. The heat of her body seeped through the thin fabric of her Christmas sweater and warmed his palms.

This time, when their lips met, there was nothing awkward or half-hearted about it. Ryan kissed Holly with a fervor. He kissed her with a certainty he hadn't felt in a long time. And oh, how she responded.

Holly's lips were pliant. They were passionate. They parted to grant him deeper access. Ryan marched forward. He claimed a sweet surrender that obliterated the fumbling misstep of their first kiss.

Holly's hands clutched at his shoulders. Her body melted into his. It was intoxicating, like some long-forgotten elixir that he knew that now he'd tasted it, it would leave him aching for more. And oh, how he wanted more.

When they finally broke the kiss, Ryan felt a mixture of triumph and bewilderment. The room felt smaller. The air thicker. Instead of silence or the sounds of their heavy breathing, he heard the whimsical tunes of the cartoon and his girls singing along. It was then that the maze of feelings and responsibilities he had to navigate seemed a lot more complicated.

But as he looked down into Holly's flushed face, her eyes gleaming with a new kind of clarity, he realized something monumental. Maybe this chaotic, awkward, breathtaking journey was a path he needed to take. Maybe, just maybe, there was room in his carefully regulated life for a little sweetness after all.

The lingering warmth from their kiss was like a halo of heat around them, a cocoon that Ryan was reluctant to step out of. He held Holly close, her body still molded to his, her breath a sweet rhythm that echoed his own. For a brief, shimmering moment, all the reasons he had been telling himself about why this was a bad idea slipped from his mind. He felt her hands move subtly against his back, and he took it as an invitation, a beckoning to taste that sweetness once more.

As he leaned in to recapture her lips, a chorus of high-pitched voices shattered the spell. "Ms. Holly, are you going to be our new mommy?"

His daughters stood in the entrance to the kitchen, eyes as wide as saucers, their innocent question reverberating like a tolling bell in the room. Holly blinked as if she'd been abruptly awakened from a dream.

The weight of reality descended on Ryan like a storm cloud, blotting out the intoxicating sunshine of the moment before. He released Holly, creating a physical and emotional distance that felt like a chasm.

"Girls, we were just—uh, discussing the new recipe," he stammered, aware that he sounded as convincing as a man caught red-handed.

Holly took a step back, her face flushed, her eyes avoiding his. "That's right," she added softly, "just working on the holiday menu." She looked at his daughters and forced a smile. "Who's ready to try out our recipes?"

The girls lifted their hands into the air, then scrambled into the high-backed chairs at the kitchen island. They both pulled a napkin from a pile and set it before them, seemingly satisfied with the deflection. But the air between Holly and Ryan had shifted, thickened with unspoken words and tangled emotions.

His daughters' innocent question rang in Ryan's ears, conjuring up images of family breakfasts, laughter, joy, and Holly as a part of all of it. But as quickly as the images appeared, they fractured, clouded by the complexity of his responsibilities, his past, and the impossibility of the situation.

Holly looked up at him then, her eyes searching his, as if trying to make sense of the collision of worlds that had just occurred. He wanted to reach out to her, to pull her back into the safety of his arms. But he felt shackled by an array of emotions he couldn't yet identify.

"I should get going," she said, her voice tinged with a sadness that clutched at his heart.

"Yeah," was all he managed to say, his voice barely above a whisper.

As Holly grabbed her coat and made her way to the door, Ryan couldn't shake off the sensation that something monumental was slipping through his fingers. He knew he should say something, anything, but words failed him.

And so, with a soft click of the door, Holly stepped out into the chilly night, leaving Ryan alone with his tangled thoughts and a lingering sweetness that felt like both a promise and a regret.

CHAPTER NINE

The room buzzed with holiday excitement, its walls adorned with twinkling lights and colorful streamers. Volunteers bustled about, wrapping toys and arranging them in piles for distribution. Holly stood with Felice and Joy, each absorbed in a conversation as vibrant as the decorations surrounding them.

Joy carefully peeled a strip of tape and secured the wrapping around a Star Voyager toy. "So I reconnected with Lucas. We had coffee, and we're having dinner this weekend."

Lucas had been Joy's first friend outside of the Evergreen family. He'd been her first crush. Her first date. Her first love. When he'd chosen to leave the valley for a promotion, and in effect break up with

Joy, it had devastated her. For years, Joy had only dated losers with no job prospects. If a guy even gave a hint of career advancement, Joy tossed him out of her life. But it had been years since Holly had seen that kind of smile on her cousin's face.

"That's wonderful." Felice grinned, finishing up her wrapping job on a plush toy. "I always said it's never too late for love."

"Okay, Felice, your turn. How are things with Mike?" Joy asked, passing the wrapped toy to a volunteer.

Felice flushed. "Good. He's nervous about the caroling concert due to his hearing loss. But I'm telling him we'll find a way through it together."

Just in time, Felice had found the baritone of her dreams. And not just for the choir. She'd enlisted Mike Harrington to do some private duets with her, and the two struck a harmonious sound the likes no one in Honor Valley had ever heard.

"And?" Joy prompted.

Felice sighed, "I think I'm falling for him."

Both cousins then turned their eyes on Holly, faces expectant and glowing. Felice dropped her ribbon. Joy momentarily halted her wrapping endeavors.

"So Holly, what's new with you? Any love in the air?" Joy probed.

Holly felt a swarm of butterflies take flight in her stomach. "I kissed Ryan," she admitted, the weight of her words hanging in the air.

"You did what?" Felice's expression was a mixture of shock and elation.

"Yeah, it happened," Holly continued. "The first kiss was, well, awkward. It was my fault. I surprised him. I don't know what came over me."

"The Christmas spirit," said Joy, waggling her eyebrows.

"But then he took charge, and the second kiss was... different."

"Different how?" Felice asked, leaning in.

"Like staggeringly different." Holly sighed, her eyes growing dreamy as she replayed the kiss in her mind. "For a moment, I even considered that maybe he's right about my recipes needing less sugar."

"That good?" said Felice.

Holly nodded.

Joy shook her head. "Holly, one good kiss shouldn't make you reconsider your culinary philosophy."

"No, it's not that," Holly clarified. "It's just that his

kiss was so... convincing. It's making me question things I never thought I'd question."

Felice leaned closer, locking eyes with Holly. "If a man's kiss makes you reevaluate some areas of your life, he's a keeper in my book."

The atmosphere grew contemplative as each cousin got lost in her thoughts, contemplating love, choices, and the whirlwind of feelings that the holiday season had stirred up.

"This Christmas is turning into a real rollercoaster." Joy finally broke the silence.

Holly nodded, her thoughts inevitably drifting back to Ryan. The sensation of his lips, the complex blend of assurance and hesitation she'd seen in his eyes. It was all incredibly compelling.

Felice tied the final bow on her wrapped gift. "Christmas is always a rollercoaster. This year, the stakes are just a bit higher."

The stakes were higher, the choices more daunting. But for the first time, Holly found herself wondering if perhaps the risk would make the reward all the sweeter. She had no idea what her next move with Ryan should be.

Should she call him?

Should she wait for him to call her?

Was she ready to be Rose and Lily's new mom?

Holly wasn't sure. What she was sure of was that she wanted another taste of Ryan.

Standing in front of her refrigerator later that day, Holly found herself eying a bag of ripe berries. She'd never used fruit by itself to sweeten one of her dishes. But what if…?

Holly pulled out more ingredients. Soon the aromatic blend of vanilla, cinnamon, and the slight tang of ginger accompanied the fresh berries. The warm lighting spilled over the wooden countertop, illuminating her bowl of freshly whipped cream and a stick of melted, unsalted butter. But the berries would be enough for the whipped cream. There was a bag of stevia in the cabinet.

Did she dare?

A whir of excitement and doubt turned in her stomach as she considered adding the sweetener to her recipe. As the whisks of her hand mixer blended the mixture into a dough, her thoughts drifted back to Ryan's compelling argument and that impassioned kiss.

The kitchen door creaked open. Holly turned, expecting one of her cousins. Instead, her brother sauntered in.

"Smells good in here." He grinned, his eyes meeting Holly's.

"Garland?" Holly exclaimed, her face lighting up. "You're here. You're early."

"I'm hungry," Garland said as he snatched her up into a big, brotherly bear hug. "What are you up to? Baking, as usual, I see. But what's this? Are you changing up your famous cookies?"

"A little," Holly admitted, her cheeks warming as if she were betraying some family secret.

Garland picked up the bag of stevia, eyebrows arching in disbelief. "Stevia? Really, sis? If I didn't know any better, I'd think Ryan got to you. The guy's obsessed with sugar substitutes."

Holly chewed at her lip, wondering exactly what she should tell her brother. But what was there to tell? "I'm just experimenting with some healthier options. That's all."

Garland shrugged, still chuckling. "Well, as long as you're not changing too much. Some things are perfect just the way they are."

He wandered out of the kitchen. If only Garland knew how close he was to the truth. If only he realized how deeply Ryan had already affected her.

Holly's hands resumed their work, mechanically shaping the cookies and placing them on the baking sheet. Her mind was far away, entangled in a labyrinth of questions, fears, and desires.

Could she really find a balance between her own traditions and the new flavors that Ryan had brought into her life? And was it only her recipes that needed reevaluating, or was it time to reassess the ingredients of her own heart?

She slid the baking sheet into the oven. The warm whoosh of air greeted her like an old friend, albeit one that carried with it the scent of something new. As the oven light cast its soft glow, Holly felt both comforted and disquieted, wondering if change —whether in a cookie recipe or a relationship— wasn't such a bad thing after all.

CHAPTER TEN

*T*he soft glow of the unicorn-shaped nightlight cast whimsical colors over the girls' bedroom. Pinks and purples danced across their walls, which were filled with framed drawings and kindergarten certificates. The scent of lavender from the essential oil diffuser mingled with the comforting aroma of the oatmeal cookies they'd baked earlier.

"You did good, Daddy," Emily said, snuggling under her Dora the Explorer comforter.

"Yeah, dinner was yum-yum," added Lily, her tiny fingers clutching her teddy bear.

A warmth spread through Ryan's chest at their words, a satisfying pulse that went beyond the simple mechanics of a balanced meal. Tonight's dinner had been a compromise, quinoa mixed with their favorite veggies and just a hint of cheese— enough to tingle their taste buds but also sneak in the healthy stuff. And it had worked.

"Thanks, munchkins," he replied, brushing a stray lock of hair away from Emily's face.

"Is Ms. Holly gonna be with us more, Daddy?" The question came from Lily, her eyes a bit too curious, a bit too aware for a such a young child.

He hadn't been dreading this question. He hadn't been looking forward to it either. But the girls were the only ones he could talk with about Holly.

Ryan wasn't close to anyone at work. He could've confided in Lucas, but the man was spending most of his time with Joy. And Lucas was a friend of both Holly and Garland. Ryan wasn't sure what he was prepared to say to either of those two Evergreens.

So, instead, he confessed to his daughters. "Ms. Holly is a very nice lady, isn't she?"

"She's the best," agreed Lily.

"She's been helping us, hasn't she?"

Emily bobbed her head. "Her apples were the best. I liked your berries, too, Daddy. I really liked them together."

Ryan had tried the two dishes together, and they'd been delicious.

"Can she be our new mommy?" Emily looked up at him with those wide blue eyes, so much like her mother's.

Ryan's throat tightened at the thought, conflicted by the tug-of-war between his heart and his sense of propriety. "Let's say our prayers, okay?"

Both girls nodded, their small hands coming together as they began their nightly ritual. "Dear God, thank you for our food, and our home, and our daddy," Emily began.

"And Mommy in heaven," Lily added softly, her voice a whisper against the still air.

Ryan's eyes stung, the moment anchoring him in a past both beautiful and painful, while teasing the potential of a future he'd been unwilling to consider. "Amen," he concluded, leaning down to kiss both on their foreheads.

As he stepped out, gently pulling the door closed behind him, the hallway seemed both a physical and metaphorical space—a place suspended between where he'd been and where he was going. For the first time, he found himself contemplating the shape of his own desire and loneliness, the empty space beside him in bed, the lack of adult conversation and companionship.

Holly could fill those gaps. She had the guts to

challenge him. She would look him in the eyes and defy him when he was being too rigid. Yet, she was also willing to listen, to yield, to seek compromise—just like last night's meals.

He had to admit it. He was attracted to Holly. Attracted to the possibility of a life with her in it, of shared breakfasts and midnight talks, of arguments and reconciliations, of love.

Ryan's hand slid into his pocket. His fingertips brushed against his phone. He thought about calling her, then hesitated. It wasn't too late. The world was quiet, perhaps too quiet for confessions. Or maybe it was exactly the right time.

Still wrestling with his feelings, he took a step toward his own bedroom. Every step seemed to echo with a silent question: Was he moving away from his past or stepping into his future?

As he lay down in his empty bed, staring at the ceiling, it struck him. Maybe, just maybe, it was okay to consider the latter.

Reaching over to the nightstand, Ryan picked up a picture of his late wife. Christine's smiling face shone back at him in the dim light. He stared into eyes that had once held all the promise and dreams of their joined future.

A pang of sorrow gripped him. It was a wound

that had scabbed but never fully healed. Tonight, for the first time in a long while, that sorrow mingled with something else: a glimmer of hope, the promise of new beginnings.

Setting the frame back on the dresser, Ryan knew it was time to let go. Time to step into whatever life had in store for him next. And that life was increasingly hard to imagine without Holly in it.

Summoning courage, he grabbed his phone and dialed the Evergreen house. His fingers fumbled a bit, his nerves betraying him. He'd dialed this number countless times over the years, but tonight, it felt like he was crossing an invisible line. The phone rang, the sound echoing in his ears, marking time and fate simultaneously.

"Hello, Evergreen residence," said a familiar male voice, catching Ryan off guard.

"Garland?" Ryan stammered, his pulse quickening. "How did you— When did you get back?"

"Just rolled in, man. How'd you know to call?"

Ryan hesitated, the silence stretching thin between them. "I didn't know you were back," he finally managed, choosing his words carefully. "I was actually calling to check in on the family."

"That's good of you, bro. You're the most decent

guy I know. You make me look bad. How are the girls?"

Ryan dutifully told his best friend about his daughters. There wasn't much to tell. He was still getting to know the girls himself. When he arrived at the tale of last night's dinner, he worked in the fact that Holly had come over to cook for them.

"She didn't tell me that," said Ryan. "But it makes sense. She was using stevia in her whipped cream."

"She was?" Ryan couldn't hide the delight in his voice.

"So you two have been hanging out?"

The pause that followed was filled with a history of friendship, of years of knowing each other, and now, of a new tension neither had yet to navigate. Finally, summoning up another dose of nerve, Ryan spoke again.

"We're just working on the menu for the base dinner together. For the children."

"Hmm" was Garland's response.

"Anyway, good to hear from you, man. We need to get together."

"Yeah. Let's do that."

"I'll let you go. Good night."

And with that, Ryan hung up the phone. His heart might be ready for something new, but he wasn't sure he was ready to make it known to everyone. Especially not his best friend who knew all his faults.

But as he sat there in the dark with the line disconnected from his friend, the certainty that he wanted the connection between him and Holly to deepen grew. Ryan wasn't sure if his desire for a relationship would cost him a friend. Would he have to give up one relationship to have the other?

CHAPTER ELEVEN

*H*olly's eyes flitted over the stacks of canned goods, boxed meals, and hygiene products, all neatly arranged on long tables. The Honor Valley holiday food pantry was in full swing. The air was filled with the comforting scent of hot cocoa and the murmur of grateful voices. Families filed through, their eyes widening at the bounty that would tide them over during the colder months. As she handed a young mother a care package, her gaze found Ryan's.

He was at the other end of the table. His muscular arms effortlessly lifted heavy boxes. His deep-set eyes met hers, holding her gaze for an electrifying second before they both returned to their tasks. There were words between them, weighty and unspoken, sentences that had been crafted but never voiced. The tension was a palpable current in the air, an unaddressed melody in a room buzzing with conversation.

Every now and then, they brushed against each other. These were deliberate accidents that sent tingles down her spine. Once, their hands met over a bag of rice, and Holly felt the simple touch reverberate through her entire being. It was a physical manifestation of the emotional and romantic chaos swirling within her.

Finally, the crowd thinned out. Volunteers started packing up to head home after a job well done. But Holly found herself rooted to the spot. Ryan seemed to sense her hesitation because he looked up from an empty box. He was in the process of breaking down and locked eyes with her.

This time, he didn't look away. They were alone in the kitchen of the base, the same place she would start cooking her meal for the base families in just an hour. Instead, he moved toward her. Each step of his boots sounded loud in her ear, a deliberate forward march advancing on his target. Holly's heart rate escalated. It knew surrender was imminent.

"Holly," he began, his voice imbued with a gravitas that made her heart skip a beat, "I want to kiss you."

The words acted like a key, unlocking a reservoir of emotion she'd been holding back. Her lips curled into a grin, almost involuntarily. All the what-ifs, the cautionary tales spun by her mind, the societal norms they were flouting—they all dissolved in the heat of the moment.

"Well, what are you waiting for?" Holly replied, her voice tinged with a playful sass that belied her racing heart.

Ryan's face lit up. In one fluid motion, he closed the gap between them, pulling her into him. The kiss was neither tentative nor rushed. It was filled with an urgency that took her breath away. It was as if they were trying to convey paragraphs of dialogue, weeks of pent-up emotion in a single, shared moment of connection.

As Holly leaned back, gasping for air, she realized that amidst the chaos of unspoken feelings and simmering tension, something simple yet profound had taken place. They had crossed a line, one she knew there was no stepping back from—and she couldn't have been happier. The ambient noise of the kitchen—a running dishwasher, the hum of the refrigerator, and the ticking of the clock on the wall —faded to a muted backdrop as Holly stood there.

"I think it's time we gave this a shot, Holly. I want to try... a relationship," he said, his eyes peering into hers like he was searching for her soul.

Her heart danced in her chest, but the euphoria was momentarily grounded by reality. "Garland—" She voiced the one name that hovered between them like a specter, making the atmosphere heavy. "How will he take this? You're his best friend, and I'm his sister."

Ryan gently cradled her face, his touch warm and steady. "I'll handle Garland. You just focus on doing what you do best—creating a fantastic meal."

Her lips spread into a smile at that. "I've actually decided to try a few of your ideas... add some of your ingredients," she confessed, her words tinged with a newfound excitement.

"We're good together, aren't we? The way we compromise."

"Compromise?" Her brows rose. "I had to drag you kicking and screaming to the sugar tin. And only then—"

And then he kissed her. Not a hurried peck or an experimental touch, but a kiss that told her, *You're my choice, and I'm willing to take whatever comes our way. Even if that's a pound of sugar.*

His lips were soft yet urgent against hers. The dual sensations were a harmonious clash that made her insides melt. When their lips finally parted, the taste of him—spicy and sweet, just like the blend of their two worlds—lingered on her tongue. When Ryan's gaze met hers, it was like a spotlight had been turned on, casting everything else into shadow.

"I'll talk to Garland," he repeated, his voice low but sure. "He's my best friend. He deserves to hear it from me."

As he spoke the words *best friend*, Holly felt a tug of uncertainty in her stomach. Garland and Ryan had been inseparable since their high school days, and the military had only fortified that bond. She wondered how her brother would take the news. Would he feel a sense of betrayal, or would he be elated that two people he deeply cared for had found happiness together?

"I've got this, Holly. Trust me."

And she did. She trusted him in a way she'd never trusted anyone before. That thought both exhilarated and terrified her.

With a lingering glance, Ryan let go of her hand and headed toward the door. "Wish me luck."

"Did you say luck or duck?" Holly made a feinting move her brother had shown her while teaching her to box.

"Funny. You're funny."

Closing the door behind him, she leaned against it for a moment. She inhaled deeply. The aromas of garlic, rosemary, and a hint of stevia swirled in the air behind her, almost like the universe was cooking up its own unique recipe for their lives. She felt like she was walking on clouds, and they were woven from dreams she hadn't even realized she'd been dreaming.

Looking at her ingredients, Holly realized she didn't have enough stevia to stretch across the meal. Picking up her purse, she headed out the door to head to the grocery store. Ryan had mentioned compromise. Well, she was about to show everyone just how good the two of them together could be.

CHAPTER TWELVE

*R*yan didn't have to go far to find Garland. As he was walking out of the door, Garland was jogging up the steps to the entrance.

"Ryan, man, what's up?"

It was now or never. Ryan cleared his throat, searching for the right words. "Garland, we've been friends for decades, so I think it's important to be upfront with you about something."

Before he could spill the revelation, Garland cut in. "You and Holly, huh? Never thought I'd see the day."

Ryan blinked. He took a step back. Then a step forward. "You knew?"

"You didn't? My sister isn't subtle. She's had a crush on you since we were kids."

"So you're... okay with this?"

"Why wouldn't I be? If my sister's going to date someone, better my best friend than some random guy."

The tension deflated like a popped balloon, and relief washed over Ryan like a cool breeze on a hot day. But it wasn't a hot day. It was the start of winter.

Still, Ryan grinned, his heart soaring. He hadn't anticipated such an effortless approval. This was a milestone, the blessing he'd yearned for, and it felt like conquering a summit that had loomed intimidatingly in the distance.

But Ryan didn't want an uphill climb. He wanted to pull Holly into his arms and kiss her sweet lips silly. So he left Garland, who gave him a brotherly clap on the back, and went back to the kitchens in search of Holly.

She wasn't there. Felice walked by humming a carol. She told Ryan that Holly had texted her that she had to make a grocery store run and would be back shortly.

There was nothing for Ryan to do but hang back in the kitchen and wait for her. The girls were in the recreational room with the other base children, engrossed in a Christmas show. The kids would be finished with their entertainments in just a couple of hours and would be expecting dinner and dessert.

Looking at the ingredients laid out on the counter, Ryan saw bags of gluten-free almond flour in place of traditional breadcrumbs for the chicken nuggets. Then his eyes landed on the pasta—infused with veggies. The curly pasta was still destined to join forces with an assortment of cheeses in what promised to be a decadent but still relatively guilt-free mac and cheese. The kale salad shone like a Christmas ornament with red pomegranate seeds scattered over the top.

Holly had listened to him. She'd respected his input. In doing so, she'd created dishes that would knock the kids' socks off and fuel their growing bodies with proper nutrition.

Ryan imagined the two of them sharing these dishes with his girls, with friends and family. Holly had given him something extraordinary today. She'd blended their worlds in the most seamless, delicious way. The only thing missing was dessert.

Most of the ingredients were laid out on the counter. He saw the huge bag of flour and the dark chocolate chips. There was no sugar to be found. The bag of Stevia was less than half full. Not nearly enough for the large batch Holly had planned to make. That was likely why she'd gone to the store.

A glance at the clock told him she'd be pushing it for time. At the far end of the counter, Ryan saw a jug of honey. It was another natural sweetener that would do what the stevia would. Without another thought, he rolled up his shirtsleeves and got to work.

Once he'd screwed off the lid, the aromatic sweetness wafted up to greet him. With an almost surgical precision learned from years in the service, he began to measure and pour the sticky liquid into the batter. However, as he began to mix, he noticed the texture transforming before his eyes—it was too wet, almost soupy.

Ryan added more flour. But then the batter became a paste. He added more honey, only to get the soupy mixture again. When he reached for the bag of flour to balance out the batter, his hand came up empty. The flour was gone.

A sudden unease had gripped him, like an itch he couldn't quite reach. Had he overstepped? The thought burrowed into his mind, undermining his momentary confidence. This wasn't just any meal; it was a meal for the children of his comrades, his brothers and sisters in arms. More importantly, it was a meal that Holly had poured her heart into, a meal that she had painstakingly planned down to the very last sprinkle of paprika.

The door to the kitchen clicked open. Holly was back. Panic and regret roiled within him. For the first time in a long while, Ryan found himself at a loss. How would he explain the liberties he'd taken with her carefully planned recipe? And even if he did, would she ever trust him in her kitchen—or her life—again?

CHAPTER THIRTEEN

*U*nloading her grocery bag, Holly felt a weight lifted off her shoulders. She had the stevia. Everything was back on track. At least it was in the kitchen. She wondered how things were going with Ryan and Garland.

That's when she saw her brother leaning against the doorway to the entrance. His eyes were twinkling in a way that she knew meant he was either incredibly pleased or up to some kind of mischief.

"Holly, can we talk?"

"Sure, what's up?"

"I just talked to Ryan. He told me you two are... an item now?"

Ryan had done it. He'd taken that step, taken that risk to potentially complicate his lifelong friendship with her brother for the chance at something more with her. It spoke volumes, and Holly found herself smiling.

And then frowning. "Where is he? What did you do to him? So help me, Garland Evergreen, if you hurt—"

Garland's laughter made Holly come to a dead stop. He pulled his baby sister into a bear hug. Holly went slack in her brother's arms. Garland had always given the very best hugs.

"Ryan's alive?" she asked, her voice muffled against his shoulder.

"He's alive and well. He's in the kitchen."

"So…? Are you okay with it? With us?"

"Are you kidding?" Garland released her and took a step back, his eyes glowing. "I couldn't have handpicked a better match for my little sister."

"You don't think he's too old for me?"

"You've always been an old soul. The age difference is nothing. But the two of you are different. It's a good different. You'll need to compromise—a lot—but those compromises will help you both grow."

Compromise had never been her strong suit in relationships. She'd always been the perfectionist in and out of the kitchen. But Ryan was teaching her that compromise wasn't a half measure in ways she never thought possible. From his dietary needs to his parenting style, Ryan was her opposite in so many ways. Yet strikingly similar in others. And according to Garland, those differences were not a liability but an asset.

"It sounds like you've thought about this a lot," she said finally.

"In the last twenty-four hours that I realized it was happening, yes. You two are like ingredients that haven't been paired together yet. Individually great, but together... potentially extraordinary."

"Good one, bro." Holly punched him in the shoulder.

"Now go finish making your dinner. I can hear the little beasts getting restless from here."

With another smile and a peck on her brother's cheek, Holly made it into the kitchen. The first thing she saw was Ryan. He had his shirtsleeves rolled up, and his forearms were covered in flour. It was the sexiest thing she'd ever seen in her life.

The panic in his eyes and grim set to his mouth didn't go well with the hot chef picture he made.

"What's wrong?" she asked. But as she looked down at the evidence on the table, she realized she didn't need an answer. "Ryan, did you do something to my cookies?"

He hesitated, his eyes flicking away briefly before settling back on hers. "Yeah, I did. I saw you were out of stevia and I thought honey might work. I'm sorry, Holly. I've ruined everything."

A complicated swirl of emotions coursed through her veins. Anger, hurt, and a tinge of betrayal mingled like the wrong ingredients in a delicate recipe. Holly felt her cheeks grow warm, and her words, usually so easy around him, felt like uncharted territory.

"All the flour is gone?"

He nodded, swallowed, and then sighed before he spoke. "I wasn't trying to undermine you. I was trying to help."

Holly's eyes darted to the mixing bowl on the counter, her stomach plummeting. The texture of the batter was all wrong. It had the consistency of cake batter rather than cookie dough.

For a moment, Holly teetered on the edge of letting her disappointment erupt. As she looked into Ryan's eyes, she saw not the confident man who could lead a hardened soldier, but a crestfallen guy who had just wanted to help. A guy who, despite messing up her recipe, had the best intentions at heart.

Her frustration fizzled.

Closing the gap between them, Holly recalled her brother Garland's words—that she and Ryan were different enough to necessitate compromise. How that very difference could be their strength if they let it. And standing there, inches from him, the aromatic blend of flour and honey filling the air around them, she felt the truth of her brother's words seep into her.

They were going to fight. It was inevitable. They were too different, too stubborn, too passionate about their respective views of the world. If every fight led to a moment like this— where their differences melted away, leaving only the raw, uncomplicated reality of their feelings— then she was ready to battle through whatever came their way.

"Hey," she said.

"Yeah?"

"I'm about to kiss you."

Ryan's lips parted, and his eyes widened.

"Are you ready?"

He managed a nod, even though he looked dazed and confused.

Holly reached up, her fingers lightly brushing the stubble on his jaw before she pressed her lips against his. It wasn't a kiss filled with passion or desperation. It was one of forgiveness, understanding, and, above all, love.

"I love you," she blurted out, her voice tinged with a vulnerability she couldn't mask.

For a moment, Ryan looked bewildered, as if he were trying to catch up to a reality that had suddenly shifted under his feet. But then, in a swift, fluid motion that belied his earlier awkwardness, he enveloped her in his arms, holding her as if she were both fragile and infinitely precious.

"I've been falling for you too," he admitted, his voice a low rumble that sent shivers down her spine. "I just didn't know how to say it, or even if I should."

"Well, you should," she said, nestling deeper into his embrace. "Because life is too short, and cookie batter is too temperamental for us not to say how we feel."

Ryan chuckled at that, the sound vibrating through her, making her feel warm and cherished. And as they stood there, wrapped in each other's arms amidst the chaos they'd created, Holly knew one thing for certain: Compromises would be made, battles would be fought, but their love? That was the one thing she'd never compromise on.

"I still ruined your dessert."

Holly shook her head. "No, you haven't ruined it.

We're just going to have to improvise. Come up with a compromise."

"How are we gonna compromise that?" He pointed to the soup mixture he'd made.

She led him back to the bowl. "This dough may be too soft for individual cookies, but it's perfect for cookie bars. We can press it into a pan and adjust the baking time. It'll be different but still delicious."

Ryan looked down at her, the uncertainty in his eyes slowly giving way to hope. "You sure about that?"

"Absolutely," Holly affirmed. "Sometimes the best creations come from happy accidents."

The tension in the room dissolved. As they got to work fixing the batter, Holly realized that this was more than just salvaging a recipe; it was a metaphor for their relationship. Imperfect, unpredictable, but wholly theirs.

CHAPTER FOURTEEN

*R*yan stood back, his arms folded across his chest as a grin stretched across his face. He watched as the kids gathered around the dining tables, their eyes widening at the festive feast laid before them. Even his girls couldn't stop grinning as they shoved the food in their mouths without a single word of protest.

For years, he'd lived in a world of duty and discipline, where the currency of survival was precision and strength. But right now, in this room filled with laughter and the scent of a home-cooked meal, he found a different kind of strength—one that came from love, compromise, and the warmth of shared happiness.

He watched as the kids bit into Holly's almond

flour chicken nuggets. The loud, satisfying crunch echoed in the room. Not a single brow was furrowed in suspicion. Not a single face puckered in distaste. Just pure, uninhibited enjoyment. Holly had managed to ensure no one had nut allergies, and now they were all blissfully ignorant that they were eating something healthy.

"Wow, this is good," said one of the kids. The others nodded in enthusiastic agreement.

Ryan shifted his gaze to the veggie pasta mac and cheese, another coup de maître by Holly. Even he had been skeptical when he'd seen the veggie-infused pasta. Watching the kids shovel forkfuls into their mouths, not an inkling of that skepticism remained. She'd pulled it off.

He held his breath, wondering how the room full of youngsters would react to the kale salad decked with pomegranate seeds. When the first brave soul took a forkful, the room fell silent. The kid chewed, eyes widening, then whooped, "It's like Christmas in my mouth!"

The room erupted in cheers. The rest of the kids dug in, their once suspicious eyes now alight with curiosity and delight. The cinnamon and vibrant pomegranate seeds had won them over. Holly had taken a room full of dubious kids and turned them into healthy food converts, all the while making it look like child's play.

Ryan's eyes found hers across the room. The laughter and chatter faded into a hazy background. All he saw was her.

His partner in crime. His equal in this chaotic, beautiful journey called life. And as her eyes met his, her lips curved in a smile that held the promise of a thousand sweet tomorrows. He knew with bone-deep certainty that whatever battles lay ahead, whatever compromises they'd have to make, they would be sweet. And he wouldn't dare ask for a substitute or alternative.

Finally, the hardened soldier within him took a back seat, allowing the man who loved and was loved in return to stand tall. It felt like liberation.

Ryan felt a gentle tug on his shirt and looked down to see his daughters gazing up at him, their eyes full of curiosity and, perhaps, a little hope. He bent down to their level. "What's on your minds, munchkins?"

"Daddy, is Ms. Holly going to be our new mommy?" they asked in almost eerie unison. The question hung in the air, laden with the weight of their young expectations.

For a moment, the room seemed to fall silent,

like the world was holding its breath along with him. He glanced over at Holly, who was mingling with some of the parents. Her laughter tinkled through the air, as light and musical as wind chimes. The way she moved, the way she lit up the room, how she'd transformed this simple meal into an event of joy—it was magnetic. And it wasn't just him; everyone felt it.

It was a simple question, really, but one that held a galaxy of implications. He'd been cautious, guarded even, with his daughters about diving into something new. The ghosts of past mistakes and unspoken regrets hovered in his mind. But as he looked into the earnest eyes of his daughters, he realized that holding on to those fears was denying them all a future that could be rich in love and happiness.

Finally, he spoke, his voice steady but tinged with an emotion he couldn't quite name. "Yes, girls. If everything goes the way I hope it will, Holly will be a part of our family."

A moment of stunned silence followed, and then their faces broke into ecstatic grins, their joy as uninhibited as only children can make it. They lunged at him, wrapping their small arms around him in a tight embrace, and he hugged them back just as fiercely.

He looked up just in time to catch Holly's eye. She was watching them, a soft smile curving her lips. Slowly, she made her way over to them. Ryan watched her movements, hungry for the moment she was close enough to bring her into this shared embrace.

And when he did bring her close along with his daughters, Ryan felt as though a missing piece of his soul had finally clicked into place. Yes, there would be challenges. Yes, there would be compromises and fights and messy human entanglements. But as he looked at his daughters' radiant faces, and then at Holly's, he knew they would face them together.

The girls wriggled free, likely to tell everyone in the room about their happy news. Now alone, Holly handed Ryan a freshly baked cookie bar. Its aroma was a heavenly blend of butter, honey, and love. Their fingers touched, an electric charge pulsing through him. In sync, they each took a bite, the sweetness of the cookie merging with the newfound sweetness between them.

"I love you," he found himself saying, the words slipping out as naturally as breathing.

"I love you, too."

Holly's eyes shimmered, and her lips met his in a kiss that tasted like promise and felt like home. It was a kiss that sealed new beginnings and second chances, one that spoke of compromise and the melding of two worlds. And as they pulled away, Ryan knew with utter certainty that he had found his perfect recipe in life—one that combined the sugar of Holly's love with the groundedness of his own being.

Don't miss the next books in the Honor Valley Holiday series!

LOVE ON A FROSTY MORNING

Two wounded hearts, one snowball fight, and a holiday season that changes everything.

. . .

Cin Evergreen was the hometown softball star whose dreams were frozen by a career-ending injury. Now she coaches middle-school kids and delights in spreading holiday cheer at her family's Christmas shop. But when it comes to love, she's always been more at home on the playing field than in the game of hearts.

Enter Derek, an ex-military sniper grappling with a life that's gone off-target. He's returned to his small hometown for peace but finds himself in the line of fire when his sister drags him to Cin's Christmas tree lot.

When Cin organizes a town-wide snowball fight, it's Derek who ends up in her sights. Sparks fly as they're pitted against each other in a frosty battle-field, and soon neither can deny the growing heat between them. But just as they start to find their rhythm, life throws a curveball that puts both their hearts on the line.

. . .

Can Cin and Derek move past their injuries and insecurities to take a shot at love? Or will they be yet another casualty of the battles they've fought? Find out in this balling holiday battle where a Wounded Warrior and the town tomboy learn they don't have a snowball's chance of escaping the Christmas spirit!

Love on a Frosty Morning **is a part of the Honor Valley Holiday romances; a heartwarming, small town, military romance series that explores the power of love, growth, and healing set during the most magical time of the year! These stories are short and sweet -the perfect length for an afternoon pick me up or an evening escape before bedtime!**

LOVE ON A SNOWY EVE

*T*wo hearts, one gingerbread house: This Christmas, love is the secret ingredient.

. . .

Ginger Evergreen has her eyes on a prize sweeter than any gingerbread house: inheriting the annual Gingerbread House Competition from her retiring mother. There's just one problem—Ginger's whimsical approach has never been taken seriously by the adults in her quaint little town.

Keith Mauro is a Facilities Engineer at the military base and a stickler for structure and precision. Missing the gingerbread competitions he used to relish with his late father, Keith is hesitant but intrigued by the prospect of partnering with Ginger. She's all tinsel and glitter. He's blueprints and calculations. When they agree to combine forces for the sake of winning, sparks fly high enough to set the roof of their gingerbread house on fire.

With Keith's strict plans and Ginger's boundless creativity, will their gingerbread house survive their competing ideals? And will this blossoming romance come out fully baked or come crumbling down? Dive into this cozy Christmas tale to find out how the magic of the season brings together two people as contrasting as peppermint and gingerbread, teaching them that the best creations often come from mixing the unexpected.

Love on a Snowy Eve **is a part of the Honor Valley Holiday romances; a heartwarming, small town, military romance series that explores the power of love, growth, and healing set during the most magical time of the year! These stories are short and sweet -the perfect length for an afternoon pick me up or an evening escape before bedtime!**

LOVE ON A HOLY NIGHT

*W*hen love and lights collide, two wounded souls find their way through the darkness.

.   .   .

Clove Evergreen is the queen of Christmas in Honor Valley. Passionate about community and connection, she has her eyes set on winning the neighborhood Christmas Light competition—earning nationwide acclaim and prize money for military families' programs. There's just one problem; the darkened, lightless, soulless house across the street where her nemesis lives.

Miles Winston, a military sniper haunted by a life-altering mistake, lives across the street from the brightest house in the neighborhood. He wants no part in the light show when he'd prefer to remain shrouded in darkness. Too bad his neighbor is determined to cast him in the spotlight, pinning him with those enigmatic eyes of hers and stealing his breath with those shining smiles. But Miles isn't prepared to let go of the shame that has made him cling to the shadows. Not even while Clove keeps showing up trying to drag him into the light.

.   .   .

Despite their growing attraction, the friction between Clove's luminescent optimism and Miles' muted sorrow creates an emotional tug-of-war. Clove believes that light and love can heal all wounds, while Miles wrestles with the notion that some scars are too deep for any brightness to reach. Their contrasting worldviews reach a boiling point when Clove's well-intentioned attempts to include Miles in the neighborhood festivities backfire, risking their burgeoning relationship and forcing them to confront whether they can ever truly reconcile their differences. Will they find a way to merge their worlds, or will they remain prisoners of their past, one bathed in light, the other in perpetual shadow?

Love on a Holy Night is a part of the Honor Valley Holiday romances; a heartwarming, small town, military romance series that explores the power of love, growth, and healing set during the most magical time of the year! These stories are short and sweet -the perfect length for an afternoon pick me up or an evening escape before bedtime!

Shanae Johnson was raised by Saturday Morning cartoons and After School Specials. She still doesn't understand why there isn't a life lesson that ties the issues of the day together just before bedtime. While she's still waiting for the meaning of it all, she writes stories to try and figure it all out. Her books are wholesome and sweet, but her are heroes are hot and heroines are full of sass!

And by the way, the E elongates the A. So it's pronounced Shan-aaaaaaaa. Perfect for a hero to call out across the moors, or up to a balcony, or to blare outside her window on a boombox. If you hear him calling her name, please send him her way!

You can sign up for Shanae's Reader Group and receive a FREE NOVELLA in this world at

https://shanaejohnson.com/ReaderGroup

ALSO BY SHANAE JOHNSON

Honor Valley Romances

Soldier's Surrender

Soldier's Promise

Soldier's Courage

Soldier's Embrace

Soldier's Protection

Soldier's Triumph

The Brides of Purple Heart

On His Bended Knee

Hand Over His Heart

Offering His Arm

His Permanent Scar

Having His Back

In Over His Head

Always On His Mind

Every Step He Takes

In His Good Hands

Light Up His Life

Strength to Stand

His Grace Under Pressure

The Rangers of Purple Heart

The Rancher takes his Convenient Bride

The Rancher takes his Best Friend's Sister

The Rancher takes his Runaway Bride

The Rancher takes his Star Crossed Love

The Rancher takes his Love at First Sight

The Rancher takes his Last Chance at Love

The Silver Star Ranch Romances

His Pledge to Honor

His Pledge to Cherish

His Pledge to Protect

His Pledge to Obey

His Pledge to Have

His Pledge to Hold

a Flying Cross Ranch Romance

His Vow to Love

His Vow to Treasure

His Vow to Adore

His Vow to Trust

His Vow to Respect

His Vow to Defend

Bronze Star Ranch Romance

His Duty to Serve

His Duty to Accept

His to Fulfill

Milton Keynes UK
Ingram Content Group UK Ltd.
UKHW021818010124
435297UK00016B/790